The van had stopped . Rak felt the crate b ... ...ered to the ground with a bump. A brignt light dazzled him, then he rolled on top of his companion as the box was tipped on to its side, two foxes terrified of what lay in store for them outside the comparative safety of their prison.

"What're you waiting for?" Again the voice had a tone of kindness. A booted foot kicked the wooden side. "You'll like it out here once you get used to it, a lot better than that cramped railway embankment. It's either this or the bloomin' council will gas the lot o' you. Too many foxes in too small a place. There'd be disease to kill you off, like it did the rabbits. We're doing this for your own good. Come on, Mike, tip the box up, they won't shift otherwise."

Also by Jonathan Guy

BADGER ISLAND

RAK

The Story of an Urban Fox

Jonathan Guy

RED FOX

A Red Fox Book
Published by Random House Children's Books
20 Vauxhall Bridge Road, London SW1V 2SA

A division of Random House UK Ltd
London Melbourne Sydney Auckland
Johannesburg and agencies throughout the world

1   3   5   7   9   10   8   6   4   2

First published in Great Britain by Julia MacRae 1994

Red Fox edition 1995

Printed and bound in Great Britain by
Cox & Wyman Ltd, Reading, Berkshire

RANDOM HOUSE UK Limited Reg. No. 954009

Papers used by Random House UK Limited
are natural, recyclable products made from wood grown
in sustainable forests. The manufacturing processes
conform to the environmental regulations of the country
of origin.

ISBN 0 09 950151 1

Contents

This one is specially
for Jody, Emma,
Kate and Martyn Webb

Chapter One

*T*he dog fox had lain in the thick clump of mugwort on the railway embankment for most of the day. It was his favourite resting place, a vantage point from which he could watch the frequent rumbling and rattling goods trains easing into the sidings around the bend, as well as being able to see the gap in the rusted mesh fence up above through which humans often entered this wilderness. Children came to play here at weekends and on summer evenings, shouting and yelling as they chased one another through the dense undergrowth.

Rak, the fox, feared neither Man nor trains; he had grown up beside them. Neither had ever harmed him, he never even considered that they would. They were a part of everyday life, companionship when he felt lonely.

He liked the mugwort with its tall stems and dark green foliage, its pungent smell in a way akin to his own body odours or those of Shi, his mate, when she chose to lie alongside him from Autumn until the Spring, retiring to the well-used earth deep in the gorse to give birth to a litter of cubs. The aroma of the mugwort reminded him of her.

The steep gully began where the tunnel came out of the

small hillock, stretched on up for a quarter of a mile until the banks levelled out. Around the corner, beyond the sidings, stood the main line station, a maze of criss-crossed lines and concrete platforms, signal boxes with ever changing red and green lights, an incessant cacophony of man-made noise and earth-shaking vibrations from the trains that came and went throughout the day and night hours.

Up above the skyline, through the stunted birch and willow saplings, it was just possible to glimpse the stark outline of the inner city; a cylindrical multi-windowed, red-bricked monstrosity that towered above the featureless high-rise office blocks and flats. By night a kaleidoscope of neon lights illuminated the drabness, alternated advertising slogans which the cinemagoers and late night revellers had long since tired of reading. They scarcely gave them a glance, yet they were all part of the human herding instinct, like a television screen that flickered on and on with the volume turned down. Something that would only have been conspicuous by its absence.

An environment that never slept.

Rak had never known any other home. Raised here from a cub, he had learned from his parents how to scavenge for food up in the city above the railway. There were streets of terraced houses, crumbling property that was overdue for demolition to make way for supermarkets and factory units. Slums that had changed little over a century. Here dustbins offered a ready food supply, meal scraps, bread that was considered stale by over-fussy humans, remnants of cooked meats and convenience foods. Throwaway containers only partly empty littered the gutters. There was much for the taking.

Waste bins were easily tipped over, the PVC lids did not rattle and clang to raise the alarm, the contents could be sifted through at leisure. Occasionally a window went up when tin cans bounced and clattered, a sleepy voice shouted and had the raiding fox scuttling for cover in an untended back garden. But it was only a question of waiting until quiet returned before resuming the scattered repast.

Sometimes, well-meaning people put out food especially for the fox population; a chicken carcass or an old meat pie thrown out on to a lawn amongst scattered children's playthings.

There was always food in plenty for the foxes. And during the annual fortnight's industrial holiday when the majority of the inner-city dwellers had departed for the coast or gone abroad, when the dustbins were empty and there was no nightly sustenance left out in the gardens, then there was always the council refuse tip a few streets away.

This strong smelling place was surrounded by a mesh fence and barbed wire to keep out humans who scavenged for their neighbours' throw-outs. But in the far corner the foxes had burrowed beneath the wire; if the council officials knew of this scratched-out entrance then they were content to ignore it. Rats were a problem, they spread filth and disease, and were not foxes, like cats, reputed to prey on small rodents? At least, the natural history books said so. In theory, then, a fox prowling around the tip was beneficial. Even so, it was necessary to bait the rats with poison in order to keep their numbers under control. Rats were a threat to the city's health, foxes were not.

Foxes harmed nobody. Over the years they had become an accepted part of city wildlife in a conservation-minded era.

Rak never troubled to chase and catch rats, neither did any of the other foxes. The cats hunted the rats, wild packs that were themselves becoming a menace within this concentration of humanity. Other cats, pets that were well fed, some of them sleek, purring creatures, docile and domesticated by day, also became predators by night. A bloodlust surfaced that had nothing to do with hunger, an age-old instinct that had enabled their species to survive.

Rak might have learned to hunt had there not been other food in abundance just for the taking. Once he had chased a young rabbit through the brambles on the embankment. He caught it and it had squealed pitifully in his jaws. He had let it go, not out of any act of compassion, simply because he could not be bothered to make the effort to kill live prey.

There were other foxes living on the embankment; Tika, the young dog fox, and his mate Brix, as well as Shi, Rak's own mate, and their litter of cubs, now more than half grown and fending for themselves. Here there were no territorial disputes mainly because there was no room for separate territories. Foxes bred, lived together in harmony that would not have been possible elsewhere. They multiplied because there was enough food for them to survive and the humans never harmed them. There were some more living up towards the sidings; there were getting too many these days, Rak thought idly, but there was nothing he could do about it. So long as there was enough food to go round then it was all right.

There were other occupants of the embankment besides foxes. Lately, though, Rak had not seen any rabbits. Either they had moved on elsewhere or they were spending all their time in the big warren beneath the mass of briars by the tunnel entrance. He vaguely recalled the last time he had seen a rabbit. It had been squatting close to the railway line, had not even moved when a train rumbled by. Usually rabbits scampered for cover when they heard a train coming through the tunnel.

There had been something decidedly odd about that rabbit.

4

It didn't look right. Its head was swollen, almost half as big as normal, and thick puss oozed from its eyes and nose.

Rak had not set eyes on a rabbit since that day. Perhaps the pair of stoats which inhabited that broken drainage pipe had killed them all. The stoats spent most of their time hunting. Rak had come to recognize the cry of a doomed rabbit, that awful squealing which embodied terror and hopelessness. When a stoat confronted a rabbit, the latter just froze into immobility, let the predator sink its teeth into the back of its neck, screamed until it died. It made no attempt to struggle or flee.

There were rabbits in hutches in some of the back gardens, too. Fat, tame creatures that did not know the meaning of freedom. They were fed, they did not want anything else in their life of imprisonment.

A couple of hedgehogs lived amidst the undergrowth. Tika had surprised one in his playful cub days and it had curled itself into a ball at his approach. He had sniffed at it out of curiosity, then yelped in pain when one of its spines pricked his nose. After that he had kept well clear of hedgehogs. They minded their own business, they did not interfere with any of the other creatures, slept in a pile of leaves for most of the winter months.

There were always cats about these days, more than ever before as they bred unchecked. All sizes and colours; sleek, well-groomed ones from good homes and scruffy, mangy ones that hunted in packs. The sparrows and the song birds which had once been plentiful here were fewer as a result of their hunting. But the cats never seemed to bother with the twittering, quarrelsome starlings. If anything, the starling numbers were multiplying. At dusk they flew back from wherever they had been feeding during the day, mostly on the refuse tip, black clouds of them that roosted on the ledges of the older buildings. Their droppings streaked the stonework white; they made more mess than all the pigeons in the big square.

Rak did not worry unduly about any of the other creatures which lived alongside Man in this congested environment. Except the dogs.

The dogs were becoming too many for comfort, almost rivalling the cat population with their prolific breeding. Nowadays the foxes had to be constantly on the alert. Basking in the warm sunshine had its perils, particularly when the dogs roamed in numbers.

The big black Alsatian-cross-Collie was the worst, a wolf-like creature with pointed ears that lay flat on his head when he scented fox. Had it not been for his resonant, excited barking then Rak and the others might have been in real danger. As it was, the dog always gave warning of its presence. On its heels, yapping frenziedly, bounded a brown and white ill-tempered terrier, a creature that had a reputation for snapping at people's heels in the streets when its futile fox hunts had frustrated it. It had once chased some children who had come to watch the goods trains shunting into the sidings. A small boy had fled screaming but nobody had done anything about it.

A brown and black dog with a tail that curled up on its hindquarters made up the canine trio, a cowardly cur that hung back when the fox scent was very strong. If the other two should corner their prey, this one would only move in for the *coup-de-grace*.

These three were the most persistent of the city's street dogs to hunt the embankment. There were others, of course, but mostly they spent their time raiding litter bins. Some were caught by the dog wardens but others took their place. Every city has its population of stray dogs.

The dogs always came through the barbed wire fence that separated the embankment from the city above, squeezed beneath the bottom strand and hunted the upper scrubland first. The foxes had long learned not to lie out in the open up there, it was too close to human habitation and its trespassers. But one warm sunny afternoon the three dogs came along the railway line, and their movements had an insidious purpose about them.

They travelled upwind of the slight breeze, kept close to the bank so that the tall wild willowherb screened them from above. The large black dog was in the lead, ears flat on its head, nose to the ground, lifting every few yards and sniffing the air for a scent. Its small cunning eyes squinted against the bright sunlight.

The terrier was close behind, perhaps the threat of angry snapping jaws curbed its eagerness. Today it neither yelped nor growled; its tongue hanging from its mouth as it panted, it wagged its stubby tail.

The brown and black mongrel slunk in the rear, clearly unhappy with this new mode of organized hunting. Far rather would it have roamed freely, hunted in the only way it knew how. This animal had no cunning; if it saw a cat, it chased it. It had never caught one, it did not expect to. Its only thrill was in the chase, it had never killed.

The black dog stopped so suddenly that its two companions bumped into it. Its head turned, its expression was a command that needed no deep-throated growl.

Meekly, the others obeyed, they knew what they must do but not why. Their leader ordered that they climb the embankment, as swiftly and as soundlessly as possible, position themselves on the slope, one a few yards below the fence, the other about halfway down. There they must remain, still and silent, with not so much as a wag of a tail that might betray their presence in the domain of the foxes.

The big dog waited until the dense undergrowth had swallowed them up before he moved on.

Rak and Shi were lying within a few yards of each other. Both appeared to be dozing in the warmth but an occasional movement of a pointed ear revealed a wariness that never slept. Noses twitched, they relied upon scent as much as sound to warn them of danger.

Usually there was neither sound nor smell to alarm them as they lay downwind of the boundary fence from which danger always came.

Except today.

Rak started, came to his feet in alarm as the wolf-like head of the black dog thrust out of a patch of mugwort, jaws dripping saliva. The small eyes bespoke the cunning and cruelty of a beast which had successfully stalked its prey. The swishing of the long stems as they sprang back into place came too late as a warning.

The dog barked just once, moved into the clearing with a casualness that was far removed from the pursuit of foxes; as if it was satisfied, as if its motive was nothing more than a stalk, pitting its skills against those of the creatures of the city's wilderness and it had no wish to harm them.

Shi leaped up, looked to her mate for guidance, noted his hesitancy, his surprise because the dogs had not come downhill the way they always did.

Rak snarled a warning but he knew that it would go unheeded, a token protest at this invasion of his homeland before he turned, leaped away in the opposite direction.

The vixen followed, heard the dog behind them. Its slowness worried her for usually the other chased them at speed, barking and snarling. The foxes always outdistanced it, gained the safety of their deep lair well ahead of their pursuer, listened to the other's frustrated howling above ground. There it would be joined by the terrier and the mongrel in a frenzied chorus. Although the terrier would threaten to go below ground, sometimes venturing inside the main entrance, it was a show of bravado; without its companions it was a coward, a mere street scavenger. The other two dogs were too big to enter the earth.

But today the dog was loping, not running. There was a chilling difference about those monotone barks as if it was signalling the direction of the chase to some unseen canine hunters.

Both Rak and Shi wondered subconsciously about the whereabouts of the terrier and the brown and black dog with the curled tail. Perhaps they had stayed at home today, found a dustbin full of edible rubbish that was far more enticing than the futile pursuit of foxes on the embankment.

Suddenly, the foxes saw the other two dogs. The terrier was above them, a bundle of seething brown and white fury, tensed to spring from the higher ground. The mongrel dog barred their way, growling threateningly.

Rak came to a standstill, Shi trembling at his side. Beyond the mongrel was their earth, their underground refuge. Their escape route was cut off; the terrier was poised to jump down on to them, and they could hear the black dog crashing through the undergrowth; any second it would be upon them. The foxes had fallen into a cunning trap set by the evil Alsatian-cross-Collie.

Rak glanced from the mongrel up to the terrier, watched as the big dog emerged from a clump of gorse, its black coat flecked with sweat. It stood there panting; its prey was trapped, there was no hurry. This was a moment in which to savour the downfall of a hated foe, one who had eluded it on many a chase. Not just Rak but his mate, too. A double victory for the price of one chase.

Time seemed to stand still for Rak and his mate. He thought about making a dash downhill, perhaps they might make it as far as the railway line, cut back and elude the

9

dogs in the mass of blackberry bushes and wild broom, reach the safety of their earth by a detour.

It was a possibility – except that right now there was a train lumbering through the tunnel.

The black dog moved a step closer, the mongrel stood its ground. Above them the terrier was preparing to launch itself on to the foxes' unprotected backs.

Then something moved in the long, dusty dry grass between the foxes and the mongrel. All of them heard the creeping rustling before it was drowned by the noise of the approaching train. The grasses parted, a grey shape with bulging, sightless eyes cowered on the well-worn track. Blinded and deafened by the disease that was ravaging the rabbit population of this place, it sensed the danger which it could neither see nor hear. It crouched, frozen into immobility by its terror, awaited a merciful release from its suffering.

The dogs saw the rabbit, tensed. Prey that was food; an easy catch for there was no place for the rabbit to flee even had it been in good health and speedy.

For a few brief seconds the cornered foxes were forgotten.

The mongrel was nearest, it knew that it could seize and kill the helpless rabbit, run with it clamped between its jaws before its companions could reach it; maybe escape with it to some place of seclusion to feast at its leisure.

The mongrel leaped forward, caught the squealing rabbit even before the terrier was airborne. The black dog barked, ran forward.

Rak's jump carried him clear of the brown and black dog, Shi was close behind him. The track veered to the right and they twisted with it in full flight, ran up the slope to where the entrance to the earth was hidden in the gorse.

Way behind them, Rak and Shi heard the dogs quarrelling over the rabbit. Deep in the safety of their underground home, the two foxes lay trembling together. The danger was past. It was all a kind of game, the thrill of a hunt. No dog had ever caught a fox down by the railway. No dog was likely ever to do so. But from now on they knew that they must not underestimate the cunning and determination of the hunting dogs that came here from the city above.

Chapter Two

*T*he animals on the embankment knew the various seasons more by a change of atmosphere, an instinctive feeling, rather than by any perceptible change in their environment. The greenery was never lush, lifeless leaves coated with a film that came from the constant pollution by the traffic; sometimes leaves fell during Midsummer, brittle and furled, a bush or tree bared of its foliage, struggling to survive. Somehow it did survive, came into bud again when the Winter was over and the weather turned warmer. Snow usually fell as sleet in the warmth of the city, or when there was a covering it melted within a few hours, turned the ground into a slushy quagmire.

Spring was when the females of the various species gave birth and the scrubland hinted at a new growth. In Summer, when the weather was hot and dry, the soil became powdery; a shower of rain turned it to mud and then the sun baked it hard, cracked it. Only the mugwort and the willowherb with its pink flowers seemed to thrive. Lately, the gorse had begun to die, a mass of spikey brown dead foliage but the bushes still provided an invaluable sanctuary for the foxes from the hunting dogs. The bramble leaves had taken on a greyish hue, the fruit was small and hard, withered rather than ripened. It was as though this small acreage within Man's domain was giving up the struggle.

The lengthening or shortening of the daylight hours was also a guide to the seasons. But, most of all, Rak knew that Autumn had arrived by his need for a mate. Shi did not scream for him as did her counterpart in the wild. There was no need in this confined area for the two of them were never very far apart. He sensed when she was ready, knew that the next cycle was about to begin.

Now they lay basking in the weak Autumn sunshine among the mugwort. Shi lay close against Rak, closer than she had lain since last year because now they had a need for each other that transcended companionship.

A train came out of the tunnel, ground noisily to a halt, waited with its engine running. A few minutes later it bumped forward, the long line of trucks rattling, stopped again. Another jerky start. Finally it was out of sight round the bend. There would be more arriving at intervals, it happened all day long, often during the night hours as well, all part of Man's mysterious lifestyle. The foxes had no idea what purpose these trains served, they weren't interested. Suffice that they came and went with regularity and posed no threat to the foxes' existence.

Rak stared at the tunnel; that circle of blackness that extended into the big mound came out again a few hundred yards the other side. Once, when he was an adventurous, inquisitive half-grown cub, he had explored the tunnel. It had been a traumatic experience. The memory of it lingered, still frightened him.

He had ventured a few yards inside, had not intended to go much further. The darkness itself hadn't frightened him, in a way he found it comforting after the semi-night gloom of an iridescent city. It was the starkness, the smooth brick-work, the artificiality that disturbed him.

He had been on the point of running back to the only environment he knew when he had heard the shrill warning hoot of an approaching train. Coming from behind, out of the sidings, as trains sometimes did at night. There was no way back, he must flee or else be crushed by the oncoming monster.

He fled blindly at full speed on up that seemingly never ending gloomy passageway with its curved roof that dripped condensation like a shower of rain. Now the tunnel was lit up as the beams of the approaching train reflected on the walls. He ran till he thought his heart would burst, until finally he emerged into that familiar murky glow cast by the surrounding city.

That was when his terror reached a peak. Not because of the oncoming goods train which was fast overhauling him, there was just room enough now to escape its churning, grinding wheels. He had expected to find an embankment, a sloping area of wasteland similar to that which he had left, mugwort and willowherb and patches of gorse in which to hide, to lie up in and take stock of his new surroundings. But there was nothing but a high blue brick wall that went on and on as far as the eye could see, not so much as a sprig of wilted greenery clinging precariously to it.

He panicked, leaped one way, then the other, wide-eyed with fear as the train picked up speed, passed within inches of him. He shuddered with its vibrations, shivered with the rush of cold air that ruffled his matted fur, then sank down exhausted as it rumbled on its way, left him quivering on the gravel by the humming steel tracks.

It had taken all Rak's courage to return back the way he had come, afraid in case he should meet with an oncoming train. Once safe back in the only habitat he knew, he had gone to ground and remained there for two whole days and nights, had gone hungry rather than go abroad to search for food.

But at least they knew what lay beyond the tunnel, a stark environment where there was no place for foxes or any other wild animals. In the opposite direction, around the bend, were the sidings and the big station with its concrete platforms crowded with humans, lights that changed and flashed by day and by night. All that remained for the foxes was this patch of scrubland. They had to stay here because there was nowhere else to go.

Shi was concerned about the increasing number of foxes on the embankment now. Up until a couple of seasons ago the earths beneath the gorse and the brambles had been sufficient to accommodate the fox population of this place. Now some of the foxes born last Spring had dug out a new home in the top patch of willowherb. Here there were no sharp thorns or spines to offer additional protection. If the dogs were persistent enough, they could dig down to their prey; if that yapping terrier found the courage there was nothing to prevent him entering the holes. But he was too much of a coward. All the same, a few breeding seasons hence there would not be room enough for the foxes here; they would be crowded together like the starlings and pigeons that roosted on the buildings at dusk.

Rak knew that she was right but there was nothing that they could do about it. Perhaps one night, when he went foraging the streets for food, he would explore further. Perhaps there was a tract of waste ground somewhere which the foxes had not yet found. If so, then he would take Shi there to have her cubs in peace. Tonight, or perhaps tomorrow, he would travel beyond his usual boundaries, take a look around. Sometime. He was not as adventurous now as he had been in those days when he had gone down the tunnel.

He felt his mate stiffen against him, knew that her ears had flicked up. She was alert, listening, perhaps she had heard something which had escaped his usual vigilance. He glanced sideways, saw her staring up the bank, watching intently. He followed her gaze but he could not see anything through the tall stems which were already beginning to shed their yellowing leaves.

Then he felt the vibrations, a faint shaking in the ground. Footfalls. Human, rather than dogs, because the tread was heavy, booted feet, not the scratching of claws which would only have been audible if you were listening for them. Rak saw his mate rise to her feet, stand erect; tense and alert. Man had never harmed a fox on the embankment but you treated him with respect all the same. You kept your distance, went below ground until he had gone.

Shi moved in the direction of the earth deep below the gorse, stopped, half crouched. The men, a tall one and a short one, were between the foxes and their refuge. The escape route was cut off.

Rak did not hesitate, he turned, knew that Shi would follow him. The newly dug earth up in the mugwort and willowherb would suffice for now. The occupants would not mind them sharing it in an emergency; once Tika had run down into the original burrow when the dogs were after him. One favour deserved another, on the embankment it was give and take.

The taller of the two men saw them, pointed, but his companion merely nodded. The humans took little notice and that was a good sign. Seconds later Rak and Shi were disappearing down in the bowels of the earth dug by the new generation of foxes.

Tika was already there with two of his companions. They

glanced questioningly at the newcomers. Why had Rak and Shi sought refuge? Was something wrong?

It was only a precaution. Rak lay down beside Tika. You didn't take chances. In all probability the men were only after the blackberries, those few that had finally ripened and were coated with dust. Once they had gathered their harvest, the humans would leave, in all probability would not return until the Spring.

Now the men were directly above the earth. The foxes lay and listened to the movements, a clumsy tread that flattened and snapped brittle stalks. A thumping noise that startled those below caused a minute avalanche of soil in the main chamber. The animals could not work out what the humans were doing. Anything out of the ordinary was frightening. Once some vandals had hacked down a couple of twisted silver birch saplings, the rotting trees were still lying by the fence. If the men were cutting down trees or bushes then it reduced the natural cover in this habitat. That was worrying, too.

Rak sensed relief when he heard the men moving away; whatever they had been doing, they had finished. Shi glanced questioningly at him and his answering expression said that there wasn't anything to worry about. But, for the moment, they would stay where they were. After dark Rak would go and search for food and whilst he was away, Shi could return to their own home.

Perhaps, whilst he was foraging, he would make a swift reconnaissance to see if there was any other wasteland not too far distant. If there was, and it was not already overpopulated by foxes, then he would suggest to Shi that they moved home. There were too many foxes living on this embankment and, also, dogs were beginning to hunt it too frequently for comfort.

The foxes dozed, waited for nightfall.

Rak heard the barking first, a frenzied, excited yapping that jerked him out of his half sleep, had every nerve in his lithe body trembling. He bounded upright, stood there listening. He was aware that the others were rousing, sensed their fear.

But there was nothing to be afraid of, rarely did a day pass without dogs venturing on to the embankment. Once they had contented themselves with rabbit hunts but now the rabbits were scarce. Rak reminded himself that no fox had ever been harmed here by a dog, it was all a kind of game. That stupid terrier was too frightened to venture below ground and the black brute was too big to enter the holes.

But there was no resonant baying from the Alsatian-cross and that was not the yelping made by its companion, the cowardly white terrier. The snarling and yapping came from more than one animal; there was no mistaking its purposefulness, its sheer ferocity. This was a pack of hunting terriers loose on the railway embankment.

Rak smelled the sheer terror in the claustrophobic confinement of the earth, his own and that of his companions. He recalled, too, that this was not the near-impenetrable home in which he had been raised and lived for all his life, protected by thick growing gorse bushes; it was a hastily scratched out burrow made by young, inexperienced foxes who sought independence away from the older ones. That, in itself, was a disconcerting thought.

The barking was louder now, closer. For the second time that day Rak felt the ground above tremble, visualized a pack of bloodlusting terriers rampaging through the undergrowth, crazed by fox scent and seeking the entrances to the refuge where their prey crouched in fear.

Rak heard the dogs at one of the entrances; he could not be sure which one for there were a number of tunnels leading down into this place. Growling, snarling, scratching at the loose earth, snapping at one another in their eagerness to be first at the kill. He had never panicked before in his life, he had had no reason to, but he did now. He was aware how his companions scattered, bolted for the exits, pushing and scrambling up the passageways which were just wide enough to admit the body of a full-grown fox.

He fled in their wake, darted from one exit to another, called once for Shi but there was no answering bark. He heard the others clawing their way through the soft soil, would have joined his mate had he known which route she had taken, but in the heat of flight there was no way of knowing.

The terriers were on their way down now, a ferocious scrambling, any second they would be down in the bowels of the fox earth. Rak plunged blindly into the nearest tunnel; he had no idea where it emerged but he did not care so long as he escaped the hunters.

In places he had to push his way through where it was narrow, a hastily and badly dug-out escape route, he wondered how far it was to the surface. Soil spilled in his wake; at least it would impede his pursuers. Frantic now, clawing and scratching, powering his progress with his hind-quarters, gasping for breath. Then came relief as he spied a circle of orange-tinted light above, a glimpse of sky that shimmered with the reflections of the city. Any second he would be out in the open, then he would flee for the streets, his scavenging haunts, seek to throw off the terriers on tarmac and concrete.

He was vaguely aware of a criss-cross pattern that lined his view of the sky. At any other time he might have held back out of curiosity or suspicion but with the hunting pack now starting to follow up the exits, this was no time to linger. He plunged forward, and in that split second of freedom something closed around his body, drew tight.

Rak fell, felt a constriction on every limb, a sudden

entanglement that trapped his legs and head, rendered him instantly helpless. He rolled, tried to stand, but whatever held him did not loosen its grip. He attempted to bite a strand that had slid between his jaws but another was muzzling him. He kicked out but his legs were held firmly.

"Got one 'ere!" A gruff excited human voice came from somewhere close by.

"And here!" A second, excited shout.

"Watch the terriers don't get to 'em, we don't want any hurt."

A melée that was beyond Rak's frightened comprehension. Terriers were barking, men were shouting. The dogs were yelping their frustration at being restrained, crazed because they had been deprived of their prey at the kill.

Rak felt himself being lifted up, tried to snap at his captors but his jaws were trapped by the smooth, strong nylon mesh of the big purse net that had been staked out over the hole. Strong gloved hands held him by his hind legs, another was attempting to unravel the mesh from his body. By now he had abandoned his struggles.

"Drop 'im in the crate!" A curt command to the man who held him. "Two to a crate."

Rak braced himself, the descent into a square of pitch darkness brought a hitherto unexperienced sense of vertigo, a feeling of abject terror. In those few seconds he willed death in the same way that a rural fox does when cornered by a pack of hounds. He resigned himself to his fate, gave up the fight for life. Until his feet touched a wooden floor and he flopped down.

He gave a glance upwards, had a brief glimpse of the city night sky before it was shut out. Something clinked, he heard a muffled voice say, "We'll load the crates into the van now."

Only then was Rak aware that he was not alone in his cramped prison. Something moved against him, huddled in

20

the corner. He scented fox and that was no small relief. It was Tika.

Rak's relief turned to disappointment. For a second he had thought, hoped, that it was Shi. Where was Shi? What had happened to her? He had no idea what all this was about, he was too shocked even to try to reason in his own way. Man had never harmed the foxes before so why was he doing so now?

No, Rak had no idea what was going on any more than Tika did. All he knew was that they had been caught up and put into heavy wooden boxes. And now those boxes were being lifted, he heard the men carrying them grunting under the strain.

They were lowered, fell the last few inches, made a resonant clang, scraped along some kind of ridged metal surface. Another clang that echoed, vibrated.

Rak could tell by the staleness of the atmosphere, a cloying smell, that the crates were inside another container of some kind, he had no idea what.

Suddenly, without warning, there was a noise that shuddered the box and whatever it was in, a roar that reached a crescendo, settled down to a steady sound that reminded Rak of . . . no, not the trains . . . but the traffic which travelled the nearby streets. He was accustomed to vehicles on his nightly prowls in search of dustbin waste, he had no fear of cars or vans. Until now. Because he knew without any doubt that the boxes containing the captured foxes had been loaded into one of those things that ran on wheels.

Tika was pressed up against him, trembling, cowering. The vehicle began to move off, bumping down a rough track until it reached the road. The tyres swished and Rak recognised the sound of wet roads. It had been raining but that was of no consequence. All that mattered was where the men were taking them and what they were going to do to them.

He sank down alongside Tika and once again resigned himself to his fate.

The journey was a long one. The roads were very wet, water splashing up on the underside of the vehicle. Once there was a screeching of rubber, and Tika was thrown on top of Rak as the van slewed. A horn blared, one of the men in the cab shouted something angrily. And then they were on their way again, travelling much slower this time.

Rak was exhausted, in any other situation he would have slept but his fear kept him awake. Tika no longer pestered him, the young dog fox had given up too.

Rak knew that Shi was in the vehicle with them. He scented her, she was confined with one of the other foxes. At least, whatever their destiny, they would surely share it together.

The van slowed, came to a halt, the engine was left running. Doors slammed, the men had got out, were coming round to the back. Rak heard one of the crates being dragged, lifted, set down on the ground. A scraping sound, the men were muttering to each other.

"Go on, off you go, then!" There was a gruff kindliness in the command. "You'll like it a lot better out here, plenty of room, rabbits to hunt."

Then the crate was put back in the van. Rak could tell by the sound it made that it was light, empty. The foxes which had been imprisoned in it had been set free.

The vehicle moved off, picked up speed. That was when Rak became aware that Shi was no longer with them. His mate had been unloaded along with one of the other foxes, set free in some unknown, frightening environment. He scratched at the side of his heavy wooden prison, a token futile attempt to escape and join Shi. Eventually he gave up, sank down alongside Tika. He didn't care what they did to him now.

The van had stopped again. Doors closed and opened. Rak felt the crate being dragged, lowered to the ground with a bump. A bright light dazzled him, then he rolled on top of his companion as the box was tipped on to its side, two foxes terrified of what lay in store for them outside the comparative safety of their prison.

"What're you waiting for?" Again the voice had a tone of kindness. A booted foot kicked the wooden side. "You'll like it out here once you get used to it, a lot better than that cramped railway embankment. It's either this or the bloomin' council will gas the lot o' you. Too many foxes in too small a place. There'd be disease to kill you off, like it did the rabbits. We're doing this for your own good. Come on, Mike, tip the box up, they won't shift otherwise."

Rak and Tika landed in a heap on a rough unsurfaced road, lay there bemused, afraid of what lay outside the circle of blinding light. Torrential rain was already beginning to saturate their coats; they huddled together, cowered.

"I hope they'll be all right." Then one man lifted the empty crate into the rear of the van, secured the double doors.

"They'll be fine." His companion was already turning away. "They'll spend the night in the undergrowth and, come daylight, they'll soon make themselves at home."

"I hope you're right, Mike." The torch was extinguished, the men walked back towards the cab. "Two more drops and then I reckon we've done a good job."

Rak watched the departing rear lights of the vehicle until they were lost to sight, lay there in the road listening until he could no longer hear the sound of the engine. Tika pressed up against him, trembling, and he wished that it had been Shi. That way, whatever their new life was to be, it might have been tolerable.

23

Instinctively, Rak moved off the track, found a bush that still had its foliage, a mass of leaves that offered scant shelter from the pouring rain. Tika followed him.

The most frightening aspect of all right now was the darkness, pitch blackness that did not have so much as a faint glimmer of light. And the silence, too, an unrelenting emptiness that was totally devoid of traffic or passing trains. Just the falling rain, dripping off the trees and bushes.

Rak had an awful feeling that there was nothing out here besides himself and Tika, that this was an empty world to which they had been transported, one of blackness and silence where nothing else lived, a place where they would die because there was nothing here to live for.

If only Shi had been with him then perhaps it would not have been quite so terrible. But Shi was gone and he would never see her again.

Chapter Three

Sometime during the night the rain eased down to a steady drizzle, eventually stopped altogether. Rak and Tika lay beneath the soaking rhododendron bush, its boughs weighed down by the wet, listened to the steady *drip-drip*. Both foxes were saturated, shivering. Their instinct was to seek cover underground but if there were any earths, then they did not know where to find them.

They were thirsty after their long journey. They stretched out, lapped at a nearby puddle. Once their thirst was quenched they experienced pangs of hunger for neither of them had eaten during the past twenty-four hours. Rak wondered if there were any dustbins or a refuse tip in close proximity. If so, then they must wait for daylight. He could not envisage life without easy scavenging, he had never gone hungry before.

His thoughts turned to Shi and he wondered where she was. Was she, too, crouched beneath some sodden bush in an alien environment, afraid of the unaccustomed pitch darkness and the eerie silence?

Tika was young and inexperienced, stupid at times. Back

home he had been the arrogant, aggressive dog fox, now he was reduced to his true self. He was relying on Rak entirely, he might be more of a nuisance than an ally in a strange, hostile land.

Overhead the skies were clearing slowly; the thick cloud formation which had brought the heavy rain was moving westwards, leaving in its wake wispy white cirrus through which a half moon cast its wan, ethereal glow.

Rak stared around him in awe, shied from the silhouetted landscape with its patches of dark forbidding shadow. Behind the foxes was a thick wood, tall spruce that might have hidden a thousand threats to trespassers in the domain of the wild. Ahead, on the other side of the rutted road, bare fields stretched up to the skyline, intersected by straggling hedgerows. A huddle in a far corner moved; sheep that had sought sparse shelter during the storm.

Somewhere an owl hooted and Tika pressed close to his guardian. Rak tensed, he had never heard an owl before; its mournful note was disconcerting, as if it had spotted the strangers and was warning the countryside of their presence.

The wind had dropped, the night sounds were magnified in the stillness. They came from near and afar; rustlings, scurryings, a cracking of dead twigs, a low branch springing back as something pushed past it. And from the deep pine forest the owl continued to call.

Tika cowered against his companion, shaking uncontrollably. Back in the city there were noises, much louder than these, but you accepted them because you lived with them. Trains screeched deafeningly but there was nothing to fear from them. Even the hunting dogs were a part of life but you knew them for what they were, learned how to dodge them. Here, in this frightful wilderness, unseen creatures moved stealthily, crept up on you.

Rak sensed a duty to appear brave; Tika had suddenly

26

become his responsibility. He needed the younger fox; without him he would have been all alone and that was too terrible to contemplate. Rak bared his teeth. He thought about a bark of defiance but he did not trust himself to utter a sound. They must wait, watch the moonlit patches between the shadows.

Something moved close, only a yard away, rustled the damp undergrowth. A pair of tiny eyes glowed redly, watching them fearlessly.

It was so small at first Rak thought it might have been a rat or a grey squirrel like those which inhabited the big park close to the city centre. No, it was neither of these. Its reddish-brown coat glinted silver as it moved out into the moonlight, dragging its long-haired tail behind it. Ears erect, it stood watching the foxes curiously. Of course, it was a stoat. As if its curiosity had been satisfied, it moved on and was lost from view in deep shadow.

Sacko, the stoat, had seen and had no further interest in these two strange bedraggled foxes. There was something odd about them but it was no concern of his. He had more important matters on his mind, he lusted for the warm blood of a freshly killed rabbit.

Now something much bigger and heavier was moving in the undergrowth on the opposite side of the forestry road, a lumbering and snapping of dead twigs. Coming this way. Rak, bracing himself, was aware of both his own fear and that of his companion. His thoughts turned to dogs, a fierce jet-black half-bred Alsatian with slavering jaws. A terrier, not the cowardly yapping cur which he knew so well but bloodlusting bundles of uncontrollable fury like those which had infiltrated the earth on the railway embankment and driven the foxes into the nets.

Why had the foxes been caught and brought to this place of darkness and terror?

27

Rak's muzzle was uplifted, he sniffed the air for a scent. Mingled odours; fear was uppermost. A rank, unpleasant stench, he knew that it lingered from where that small creature had passed by. There was no canine aroma, that was a small relief. Then came another which he did not recognize; it kindled within him a terror of the unknown, some alien animal which posed a threat to urban foxes who dared to trespass in its remote domain.

Another movement, a loud snapping as if a heavy branch had broken beneath the weight of a cumbersome body. Tika started and would have fled had there been a safe haven behind them. Rak gave a warning snarl, which sounded more like a whine.

Then, directly opposite where the foxes cowered, a head was thrust through the leafy rhododendron screen, a white strip running down the length of the head to the pointed snout, short ears uplifted as though in curiosity, small eyes glinted, reflecting the moonlight. Watching. Staring.

Rak's terror reached a peak, he had never dreamed of the existence of such an animal, so broad and powerful as it eased into full view, as big as some of the dogs that had roamed his former habitat. Its powerful body was covered with short grey fur, its claws sharp and vicious. Whatever it was, it had surely scented the foxes and was moving in for the kill.

It stopped, watching them closely; it was clearly puzzled. Aggression was replaced by curiosity, it made no further move to advance.

Badgers are by nature curious creatures. This boar was no exception; inoffensive, it hunted these woods at night, scratching for grubs, a nest of voles if it was lucky. A young rabbit was a delicacy. Foxes were plentiful in these wooded hills, the species tolerated each other, a mutual respect existed.

Tonight Tosca, the vixen, had screeched for Rus, her mate of many seasons, and he had answered her call. The badger chose to avoid them whenever possible. Then he had picked up the sour scent of fox and, wondering why two foxes lingered here on a stormy night, had gone to investigate.

Yes, there was something decidedly strange about this pair, he was not sure exactly what. They had not sought cover during the downpour but had a forlorn rather than a majestic look about them; their coats were in poor condition, lacking the healthy sheen of the wild. They appeared terrified, something which he had only witnessed once before when a fleeting vixen had sought refuge from the pursuing hounds in the big badger sett. And there were no hounds abroad tonight, Man only hunted by day. It was very odd indeed.

Foxes and badger continued to regard one another. The distant owl had stopped hooting, the small scurryings in the surrounding undergrowth had stopped. The awful, threatening silence returned and then a scudding cloud crossed the face of the moon and plunged the countryside briefly back into darkness.

The foxes huddled together, feared a sudden charge by the fierce brute with the striped head, braced themselves for the crunch of those mighty jaws. They heard a crashing of undergrowth.

Then silence.

The cloud thinned, passed, and again this desolate landscape was bathed in silvery moonlight. Rak was almost afraid to look, scared of what he might see, an unknown beast poised for the kill. But there was nothing, not so much as a scuttling mouse or vole in sight. The badger was hungry, food was not plentiful with the approach of winter, and the night hours must be spent foraging rather than idling his time away with strange foxes who, quite obviously, were not native to these parts.

Rak and Tika relaxed a little. The badger was gone. If he was going to attack them, surely he would have done it at the time? All the same, it had been very frightening, there was no mistaking the other's hostility towards them. Did this strange land harbour any more terrifying creatures? The foxes crouched there, glancing about them in the moonlight.

They were exhausted but they dared not sleep in case something sneaked up on them, caught them unawares. They leaned against each other, from time to time their heads drooped then jerked up again. Watching. Listening.

Tika told Rak that he was hungry. Rak had forgotten all about food until then and suddenly his stomach began to rumble. He remembered those nightly forays after dustbin scraps in the fox-friendly city. Hunger was a worrying thought in an alien environment; he wondered where the streets were here, the houses with their gardens and dustbins in the alleyways. Maybe they were on the other side of that big hill opposite. At first light they would go up there and look. Exploring new territory by night was not a task to be relished.

They sensed that dawn was a long way off. Even in the heart of a city foxes learned to tell the night time by the moon. In the meantime they would stay where they were; nothing had harmed them so far, even that aggressive striped animal had gone away.

A fox barked somewhere in the wood behind; Rak started, felt his companion tense along with him. There was something disconcerting about that bark, it wasn't how the dog foxes on the embankment usually barked. Certainly it wasn't an answering call to a vixen's screech for mating; it was more like a warning.

To themselves.

They were uneasy again. So there were other foxes in this awful place. Perhaps they, too, had been transported here in wooden crates from some urban habitat. If so, then they had survived, found food. Rak was tempted to give an answering bark but something made him hold back because the other's call had been far from friendly.

Some time later Rak scented fox on the breeze, there was no mistaking that rank odour of his own species. The stranger was close; too close for comfort. He told Tika to watch in the direction of the roadway whilst he looked back towards the dark woodlands. Not that he could see much against the shadowy background, anyway.

There was a movement amongst the trees. It certainly wasn't the animal with the striped head, it was much too stealthy for that, a beast of prey that stalked with cunning, moving close until it was time to pounce. Again Rak braced himself.

Suddenly, he saw the other, a creature almost half as big again as himself, standing half in shadow so that it might have been even larger than he thought. Its very posture was regal, a majestic specimen whose coat shone sleekly in the half light, jaws agape in a threatening gesture. It stood there, some five yards away, its breath vapourising in the cold night air, watching them intently.

There was contempt in its expression; it demanded to know who these trespassers were in the territory of Rus; how they came to be here, where they had come from. Why did they skulk beneath the bushes? Why were they apparently well-fed and yet their coats were in such poor condition? Did they not know that he, Rus, ruled over this land and that no other dog foxes were allowed here whilst his mate, Tosca, screeched for the male of the species?

Rak and Tika did not know, of course. They knew nothing about territories; back in the city all foxes had been equal. There were squabbles, naturally, sometimes the males fought over a vixen at mating time. But the embankment had no ruler. All this was puzzling. There was something menacing about the big fox. The fact that he had sought them out, knew where they were hiding, was unnerving.

Rak tried to explain about their former home, how Man had caught them up, brought them here. Rus's gaping jaws seemed to smile with contempt for a lesser species. Oh, yes, it had happened before, once to his own personal knowledge and he had heard about similar instances from other foxes. Ignorant, scraggy specimens had been dumped in a land where the fox was king, a ruler over all other creatures of the wild. These lesser creatures from Man's habitat were a disgrace to a noble species. Rus flicked his brush arrogantly.

Well, he, personally, would not harm Rak and Tika. Unless, of course, they tried to usurp his rule, and that would be a very foolish thing to do. They could stay, provided they did not go near Tosca. That would mean certain death at his own jaws; saliva strung from his fangs at the thought. They must keep to themselves. He turned as if to go, satisfied that he had explained the true position of lowly relatives from a foreign habitat.

But, he added, standing in shadow now so that the watchers were unable to see his expression, to his own knowledge, he did not know of a single town fox who was still in these hills from those who had been transported here by Man. They might have left, moved on, that was a faint possibility. Most likely – Rak and Tika sensed a sneer – the town foxes had not survived.

Rus was gone as quickly as he had come, a bound that took him back into the big forest, loping away down well-used animal tracks that were known only to the inhabitants of this place.

Rak and Tika huddled together, neither was ashamed of their trembling. They stared wide-eyed at the blackness of the forest and hardly dared to imagine the dangers which it held for an unwary fox who had known only the safety and easy life of a city wasteland.

What unknown perils awaited them? Rus had delivered his warning; they were not welcome, they would be spurned by the foxes of the wild. But he, the ruler of these wooded hills, would not harm them provided they kept themselves to themselves. Maybe he would not need to, for those who had been brought here before were no longer around . . .

Rak tried to convince himself and his companion that there was nothing to fear. Maybe the other city foxes had found a habitat that was acceptable to them, where they now lived in peace and harmony.

When daylight came they would move, find food, and see what lay beyond the skyline.

Chapter Four

Sheep heads lifted up from the coarse rain-soaked grass which they had begun to graze soon after daylight. They were animals that accepted their lot in life without question, only ventured from the safe pastureland if they chanced to find a break in the rusted and buckled mesh fencing which contained them, and only then because the pasture in the adjoining field was sure to be more lush.

If one of their companions moved, they followed, neither knowing nor caring where it was going. Nervous creatures by nature, they bunched and bleated at anything which was out of the ordinary. Their only fear was dogs, the occasional stray from the village below or the ageing collie which the farmer used to round them up. Dogs chased them, barked, snapped at their heels, then herded into a corner of the field from where there was no escape.

They knew the difference between dogs and foxes, also that foxes were only a threat during the Spring, not to themselves but to a newly born or sickly lamb. There were always foxes in the fields, usually during the hours of darkness, hunting the rabbits which emerged from the woods and hedgerows to graze. They were used to the pitiful squealing of an unfortunate rabbit which had fallen prey to Rus, and took no notice because it was all part of life in the hills. It did not concern them.

Now they stood and stared, watched the two foxes coming up towards them from the rutted road below. In their own way they sensed that there was something odd about this pair. Foxes sometimes hunted during the daylight hours, mostly in severe weather when food was scarce and they were hungry, but these did not appear to be hunting. They did not quarter the grassland, noses to the ground in search of a scent, checking every thick clump of grass or thistles which might have concealed prey; they walked in a straight line, paused every so often to sniff the air, glanced nervously around as if they feared pursuit. Even a sheep, a creature of limited animal intelligence, recognised fear in a fellow animal.

The flock stood and watched the progress of the two foxes, stared after them until they were lost from view somewhere up towards the distant skyline. Then an ageing ewe resumed grazing and the rest followed. A matter of passing interest was forgotten.

Rak and Tika reached the top of the hill, flopped down. Their muscles ached, they felt almost as though their legs would no longer support their bodies. They were unused to travelling long distances over steep terrain; up until now their only ranging had been the extent of the railway embankment and scavenging forays into the city streets. Exhausted, they lay there, felt the hunger rumbling their stomachs.

They saw the land on the other side of the big hill for the first time now, a panoramic landscape that was a continuation of the one which they had just left; below them lay a valley with white-washed cottages, smoke wisping up from the chimneys, a car wending its way along the narrow road until it was lost to sight around the bends. Beyond, the land rose sharply again, a wooded hillside where firs were planted in blocks, intersected by grassy rides, until they reached the big forest that stretched right on up to the horizon.

The artificial sea of dark green was broken only by an area of mighty centuries-old deciduous trees in their midst, oaks and beeches which clung stubbornly to their dying golden leaves, and had survived the elements and thwarted Man's efforts to fell them and replace them with commercial uniformity. An ancient island in a modern landscape, proudly defying the march of progress.

This distant wood seemed to extend a welcome to Rak, as though it offered sanctuary in a wild land, a refuge from the beasts with striped heads and the regal Rus who had branded them outcasts. A habitat of his ancestors long before Man created concrete cities. It stirred something within the fox which he could not understand, temporarily eased his home-sickness and his pining for Shi.

Tika was restless. Suppose, he suggested to Rak, they started out, slept by day, travelled by night, then surely, eventually, they would reach their homeland? Wouldn't they?

Rak was tempted but they had no idea in which direction the city lay. They might, in due course, find themselves in an even more hostile land. First, they must find food, build up their strength. Then they needed to rest for a while. That wood over yonder, the mature trees towering above the sap-lings, had a welcoming look about it, it offered warmth and shelter and it was within travelling distance of the village below. They would be able to make a nightly trip down in search of food.

And, in due course, Rak would decide whether they stayed or moved on. He was determined at the outset that all decisions would be made by himself. In no way was he going to allow his inexperienced companion to influence him. They would lie up here until nightfall and then they would go and see what the village had to offer in the way of food.

They rested, half-dozing, but ears tuned in to pick up any sound which might constitute a threat to their presence in this alien land. Below them sheep bleated contentedly in the warm sunshine, moved on up towards the shelter offered by the edge of the adjacent wood as the evening approached.

Tika was impatient, his hunger over-ruled his exhaustion, the thought of food had him struggling to his feet, looking down at Rak; by the time they reached the village it would be dark enough. They had gone almost two whole days and nights without eating.

Rak bared his fangs in a command to the other to wait. They would leave when Rak decided it was time, not before; it was necessary to instil some discipline into his headstrong companion.

Tika checked, cringed an apology, and at that moment something jumped up out of the long grass at his feet. The young rabbit had lain there trembling for hours, hoped that the foxes would move on. It scarcely believed that they had not scented it. Now, suddenly, all that was left to it was flight.

An instinct that went back before the days of urban foxes springboarded Tika into pursuit. A leap, a bound overcame his dragging tiredness. He sensed Rak close behind him. But not for one second did either of them associate the fleeing coney with food; they would chase it for the same reason that the dogs back home chased the foxes on the embankment, a game that was a diluted return to their predatory heritage.

Tika's long bounds took him alongside the pursued. A sideways turn, a snap of those powerful jaws and he would have broken the rabbit's back. Instead, he raced level, even slowed his pace. Rak was on the other side; he made as if to grab for the smaller creature's hindquarters, changed his mind. The rabbit feigned left, then right, saw that there was no way he could break past his pursuers, a direct course was all that was left to him.

A hundred yards on and a line of sagging sheep fencing was silhouetted against the dusk – square mesh through which a rabbit could pass with ease. The darting rabbit found an extra spurt of energy from somewhere, a rush of adrenaline boosting it in its hour of need. It gained a yard, the foxes drew level, eased slightly ahead. They could easily have cut off its escape route but, instead, they were content to canter alongside the other. Until the rabbit hurled itself at the fence, squeezed through a square of mesh and left the foxes thwarted by the strumming wire.

The foxes pulled up. They had succumbed to a moment of playfulness at a time when they needed to conserve their waning energy. They had never even considered actually catching the rabbit, only chasing it, scaring it in the same way as they sometimes frightened the rabbits in the hutches in the city gardens. Mischief had no place in the serious business of survival.

Rak drew himself up, attempted to retrieve the dignity of a leader. It had been a respite, a bit of fun, but if they saw any more rabbits, they would ignore them. The priority was to find food.

The tiny village was as different from the city as this environment was from the railway embankment. A row of stone-built terraced cottages with side alleys dividing them, but no dustbins in the passageways. The gardens were neat and tidy, grass mowed short and not a sign of scraps thrown out. A bird table had a mesh bag of nuts hanging from it; Rak sniffed at it, decided that the contents were inedible.

In one garden there was a vegetable patch with soft soil and a heap of yellowing potato foliage left after the harvest.

Some chickens squawked in alarm from a closed shed and that started a dog barking inside one of the houses. The foxes tensed, they were even more wary of dogs since their recent capture.

The foxes moved away from the cottages, came to a large house standing back from the road. There were lights showing behind the closed curtains of a downstairs window. Rak walked along a grassy verge on the side of the long gravelled drive, Tika followed. With good reason both animals were nervous now in close proximity to human habitation. They trusted Man no longer.

At the rear of the house stood a trio of concrete dog kennels with enclosed wire runs. Rak paused, they seemed to be empty, but in any case if there were dogs inside then they would be unable to get out. Tika stood motionless, nose uplifted. He scented the dustbin even before he saw it, that familiar appetizing aroma of decomposing vegetable scraps, a whiff of decaying meat. They were in luck!

The foxes padded softly across a stone-flagged yard, saw the dustbins lined up against a brick wall. The stench was stronger now; Rak and Tika dripped saliva at the prospect of a feast.

The bins, too, differed from urban waste containers. These were not the PVC dustbins with which they were familiar, instead they were galvanized with lids that fitted snugly.

Rak stood on his hind legs, rested his forefeet on the nearest lid. The bin rattled slightly. There was only one way to dislodge the lid, the method he always used when occasionally he came up against a stubborn one on his street forays. He pushed with all his weight, jumped clear as the dustbin toppled, rolled and clanged metallically as it came to rest against the opposite wall. The lid came free as if a lever had been applied, spilled out a pile of rubbish.

Rak and Tika leaped forward and began pawing at the

sticky waste. They scented meat, a chicken carcass, some kipper remains. They pulled at it, their teeth crunched on bones, they chewed, swallowed. A repast for the ravenous, anything that was edible was acceptable.

That was when the dogs in the kennels went crazy, a trio of Alsatian guard dogs hurling themselves frenziedly at their steel mesh prison, clawing, snarling, a froth of frustration foaming from their wide jaws. They had been sleeping, the foxes had crept in unscented; the clattering of the dustbin had jerked the beasts into maddened wakefulness.

Rak and Tika turned, would have fled except that they saw that the dogs could not get to them. They resumed their scavenged meal, watching the kennels as they gulped mouthfuls of discarded kipper remnants. The Alsatians hurled themselves at the wire, fell back, jumped again, bayed with deep throated voices.

A door scraped open, a man stood framed in the light behind, he held something which resembled a stick in his hands. A woman peered from behind him, shading her eyes with her hand.

"There's somebody about, John!" Her voice was high-pitched, squeaky. She was nervous. "Don't go out there, just loose the dogs."

"Look, it's foxes!" Rak saw that the man had the stick halfway up to his shoulders. "They're raidin' the dustbins!"

The foxes would have stood their ground, defied the barking dogs, but humans now posed a threat which had been non-existent two nights ago. Rak turned, crunching on a chicken bone, ran with it clenched between his teeth, Tika following instantly.

A deafening explosion reverberated through the partly enclosed yard, followed by a second one almost instantly. Vivid flashes, reminiscent of sheet lightning, illuminated the kennels, showed the fleeing foxes those watching eyes and open jaws. A vicious whistling and pinging of leaden shot ricochetted from wall to wall.

Shot flew in all directions, a spent pellet, already flattened by the brickwork, hit Tika on the haunch; it stung but it did not penetrate the flesh. The double report of the shotgun catapulted the Alsatians into a further futile onslaught on the mesh runs. The man was shouting, cursing, fumbling to reload. But by the time the second twin shot blasts cut wildly across the spacious lawns, Rak and Tika were at the entrance gates, swerving to the right and running up the road.

They did not stop until they reached the cover of a silver birch spinney on the outskirts of the tiny village. Here they lay panting, breathless after their unaccustomed flight, trying to listen above the pounding of their hearts in case those dogs were loosed.

But there was no pursuit. Foxes were commonplace in these parts. If you were a shepherd or a gamekeeper you waged a ceaseless war against your deadliest foe, but if you were neither of these, and a suspected prowler turned out to be a fox, then your relief was such that a few wild shots in anger were sufficient.

Rak and Tika were both scared and shocked. The human threat was becoming more apparent daily but never before had they met up with deafening bangs and charges of shot-blast skimming all around them. They were lucky not to have been injured or perhaps killed, they knew that only too well. The small consolation was that they had eased their hunger pangs a little but Rak's concern was where the next meal was coming from. It was not safe to come into contact with Man; and Man had always been their provider.

He explained to Tika that they must hide, lie low, perhaps reconnoitre this menacing new environment. They might even think about that long trek in an attempt to return to their city home. But in the meantime they must find a place of safety.

Rak's thoughts returned to that tract of woodland high up on the hillside beyond the village, age-old trees standing proudly above a younger, lesser species. Even in their present predicament, the place had an appeal. It had looked so natural, almost as if they had been there before. They hadn't, of course, but it had an atmosphere about it, like an oasis to the desert traveller who has almost given up all hope.

After a while Rak and Tika left the outskirts of the village, and headed uphill where the sickly sweet scent of the pines hung heavy in the cool night air.

Chapter Five

Rak and Tika lay on the fringe of the fir forest looking at the majestic outline of those tall oaks and beeches with their mighty gnarled boles, boughs which the westerly gales had twisted into shapes that would have defied the efforts of a skilled sculptor; crooked arms with hands that beckoned, others that jutted upright in a gesture of defiance to Man and the elements.

A belt of rhododendrons grew on the outskirts of the wood, a barrier designed by Nature to impede the casual human trespasser or as a vantage point from which the inhabitants of this mysterious place could see without being seen.

Who were the occupants?

That was what worried Rak most. Especially when an owl hooted from within and he recalled how, two nights ago, its warning had summoned those creatures who had regarded the strangers with suspicion and hostility.

Might this isolated wood not be the home of Rus, his regal domain which he had warned the two foxes not to enter? Starlings shifted in their rhododendron roost, twittered amongst themselves. A rabbit which had been grazing on the strip of undergrowth which divided conifers and deciduous trees, hopped into the cover of a nearby clump of brambles.

Rak's ears cocked up, he heard a whistle of fast wingbeats, glanced skywards in time to catch a glimpse of three arrowing mallard briefly silhouetted against the starry sky. Even in his urban surroundings he had been familiar with the mysterious comings and goings of wild duck. Doubtless they were bound for some distant lake where they knew of a ready supply of food for, like foxes, they fed by night. In the big park in the city humans threw them stale bread, the birds had no need to fly off to feed, they merely flew to exercise their wings.

Rak and Tika were still hungry.

The only sound now was the soughing of the gentle breeze through the trees, the fluttering and rustling of dying foliage. Rak knew that sooner or later he and Tika would have to enter the wood opposite.

Tika slunk at Rak's heels, would never have dared to cross the strip of open ground had he been alone. His instinct was to turn and flee, the only reason he did not was because he could not face the thought of being without Rak in this wild land. Glancing from side to side, looking behind him in case some fearsome animal crept upon him, he kept his nose close to his companion's trailing brush.

They rustled the low branches of the rhododendrons; starlings, bunched together, voiced their protest at this unexpected intrusion of their roost. The ground beneath their winter home was deep with their droppings, a slushy layer that gave off a sour and pungent stench. With the coming of Spring they would disperse, some would return to the far distant lands from which they had come, others to the fields and hedgerows. This place was only a winter habitat.

The foxes emerged from the dense barrier into the wood

44

which it protected, stood and stared in awe, such was the contrast between this place and the lifeless interior of the spruce and fir forest. The oaks and beeches towered above them like statues, the ground below was a spongy carpet of fallen leaves that rustled with every footstep. Bushes and brambles, through which ran well-trodden tracks, had Rak tensing. It was as if the foxes had stepped from a desolate and unfriendly land into one which was warm and welcoming, sheltering them from the gales and lashing rain outside, a haven which Man had not infiltrated, perhaps he did not even guess that it existed. It was as though time ceased here; everything was the same as it had been in the days of their distant ancestors.

The foxes stood there, over-awed, afraid to venture any further into this mystic secret haven. Their sense of safety was tempered by a fear of the unknown, those tracks bespoke a constant coming and going of animal traffic. Rak's nose uplifted again, he smelled mingled scents, some he recognized, others he did not. It was the latter that worried him.

There were rabbits here, their scent was akin to the tame ones in the garden hutches without the aroma of unchanged wood shavings; fox, but it was not fresh, perhaps one had passed this way earlier in the day, had used this hidden wood as a daytime refuge; an unpleasant odour like the one that had emanated from the stoat, that small squirrel-like creature which had paused to survey the newcomers on their arrival; and a distinctly earthy smell that was growing stronger by the second . . .

One moment the clearing in which Rak and Tika stood was deserted, the next that fearsome striped countenance was confronting them from less than a yard away; the powerful creature had appeared silently, only its strong odour announcing its presence. Rak started, backed away but his retreat was halted as he bumped into the cringing Tika. Now

45

he could see the strange animal, he was sure it was the one they had met before; it stood half hidden in the entrance to a wide burrow, similar to the one which he and Shi had painstakingly dug in the railway embankment prior to the birth of their first litter. He experienced a brief longing for his mate, then his gaze wilted beneath the baleful glare of those gimlet eyes.

Rak was very frightened. Tika was terror stricken, cringed up against his companion. Both of them considered fleeing but this huge brute might well have chased them, and they had no idea how fast he could move in spite of his size.

The badger wanted to know what they were doing in this wood that had been the secret kingdom of the badgers long before he was born. Why had they trespassed here? Answers were demanded, questions were not to be asked.

Rak replied that they had found it by chance, two wandering foxes in a strange land who were both homeless and hungry. They did not mean to offend; if they had, then they would leave immediately. They were lost, their intention was to travel on in due course and hope to find their way back to the human habitation from which they had been brought by Man. They had not wanted to leave their home, they had had no choice. They were very homesick.

The badger was curious. How was it that foxes lived alongside Man? Surely they knew that humans hunted them, killed them at every opportunity. In these hills Man rode on horseback, used a pack of dogs to scent and hunt down foxes. Sometimes, too, the shepherds came on foot, used sticks that made a loud bang and the foxes died. But, he added smugly, Man *never* harmed badgers. This, surely, was proof that badgers were superior to foxes.

Rak agreed, you dared not disagree with a creature so fierce and dominant. It seemed to please the other, it was almost as though he smiled with his mouth. He edged right

46

out of the hole, and Rak thought for a moment that he and Tika were about to be attacked. But he sensed a lessening of the original ferocity, almost an understanding of their plight.

The badger was curious; he wanted to know more. Rak tried to explain; at one stage he thought he detected disbelief in the other's tiny eyes, then contempt. Had foxes no pride, relying upon humans for their living?

There was an arrogance about the badger, and having heard how, if not why, these foxes came to be here, whether he believed or disbelieved Rak's story, he clearly wanted to tell them about the badger colony that lived in this hidden wood.

His name, he said, was Shaf and he was the leader of these badgers. He had no real objection to foxes; he neither liked nor disliked them, but he would help them, as he would any creature in his domain, if they were threatened by Man. There were occasions when Rus and Tosca had lain low in the sett when the Hunt was in the area.

Likewise, last Winter, a pair of foxes had lived in the upper gallery, but on the understanding that they vacated it once Spring arrived; the badgers always inhabited the lower one during the colder months. The badgers would not cohabit with foxes once the breeding season began. The sett was cleaned out, the old bedding replaced with new, and the rank odour of fox dispersed. The main problem with foxes, Shaf glared his disgust, was that they *smelled*.

On reflection – Shaf's contemptuous expression was replaced with a look of condescension – he was prepared to offer his unexpected callers *temporary* accommodation. Until Spring, but he hoped that they might leave before then. They surely would as Rak had stated their intention of trying to find their way back to their former habitat in a human environment. What a strange idea, it was quite unbelievable, but if that was what they desired then it was no business of

47

his. Now, if they would care to accompany him, he would show them their quarters. They might not like them, of course, he would not be offended if they chose not to accept his hospitality.

Rak followed Shaf down the wide tunnel, Tika close behind him. The foxes were uneasy, fearful lest this might be a ruse to lure them below ground so that the badgers could trap them, rip them to shreds with those sharp claws. But there was no turning back even in this enlarged burrow, no room in which to swivel and flee back to the surface.

The air below was stale and yet there was a cleanliness about the place which Rak became aware of at once. Clean dry soil, no rotting scraps littering the ground as there always had been in the fox earth on the railway embankment. There was neither sign nor stench of foulings.

Soon they emerged into a wide gallery, a subterranean chamber that had been painstakingly excavated amidst the deep roots of the oaks and beeches which grew above.

The foxes could stay here if they wished, Shaf seemed in a hurry now. The other badgers would already have returned from their nocturnal search for food; if you listened carefully you could hear them snoring in the lower gallery. Rak and Tika listened; certainly there was a distant sound, they would take Shaf's word for it. Right now they had no wish to meet his companions.

Shaf seemed to read their thoughts. On *no* account were they to venture below, that would be treated as a violation of the hospitality offered by the badgers, who would be very angry at the disturbance. That would be the one occasion when their leader would have no control over them. There had been such an instance last season when an inquisitive half-grown fox cub had trespassed in the bowels of the sett . . .

Foxes and badgers would doubtless meet in due course;

48

usually they ignored the presence of the other species, a kind of truce which was the nearest either would come to integration.

Now, be gone in the Spring, do not linger once the trees begin to sprout their new growth!

Just one last question, Rak braced himself, the badger was becoming restless, impatient at a further delay. Rak explained that they were hungry, they had barely eaten during the last two days. Did Shaf, by any chance, know where they might find food?

The answer was abrupt, contempt again. This land was plentiful in food for both badgers and foxes. Any self-respecting fox would find a rabbit within yards of the sett but since these strangers from Man's artificial world seemed ignorant of hunting matters, Shaf would give them the benefit of his advice. Outside the sett there grew a mighty oak tree with spreading branches and beneath it was a mass of brambles. Venture into the briars and there was an extensive rabbit warren. In places where the tree roots spread and made burrowing difficult, the holes were shallow and easily scratched out. In some of them the foxes would find young rabbits which had been born late in the season, a real delicacy.

But, a final word of warning, one that Shaf had somehow overlooked; this wood was also the kingdom of Rus, the dog fox, whose strength and cunning had enabled him to survive many seasons of Man's hunting and killing with the sticks that banged. Encounter Rus at your peril, for although he tolerated badgers, no fox in these wooded hills dared to trespass on his territory. There was a fox once, Shaf could not remember his name and it was of no consequence anyway, who had come up here from the lower fir wood, a foolhardy, arrogant animal, as strong as most foxes – one had to admire his daring – but one dark night he had met

Rus upon his travels. Shaf turned away, ambled towards an entrance that sloped deeper into the ground, he really did not have the time to tell them the story of that savage encounter. Another time, perhaps . . .

Now Rak and Tika were left alone in the darkness of the badger sett. They found a corner, lay down together, and reflected upon this unexpected hospitality. Rak's instinct had not betrayed him, this wood had a friendliness about it but not in the way he had supposed. The badgers would not worry them but they must keep clear of Rus, flee if they scented another fox for it would undoubtedly be him.

They were puzzled, too, about Shaf's advice on the nearby rabbit warren. They had never really associated rabbits with food, had not troubled with them in the past except to chase them in play. But the foxes had fed on meat scraps and chicken carcasses out of the waste bins, and rabbits were meat. They only had to be caught. And killed.

Rak told Tika that they would sleep now, and when night came again they would go above ground and hunt rabbits. Right then, hungry as they were, it seemed an exciting idea.

Below them the badgers were snoring loudly. It was a soothing sound and in due course Rak and Tika drifted into an exhausted sleep.

Chapter Six

*T*onight the sky was cloudy, there was not so much as a glimpse of the previous night's scintillating stars. Rak and Tika found the pitch blackness disconcerting, they were not accustomed to a world in which they had to rely almost entirely upon scent. Standing on top of the huge mound which roofed the badger sett, noses to the wind, they sniffed for any scent which might herald danger.

The slight breeze brought mingled odours; oversweet blackberries which had ripened beyond the reach of foraging woodland creatures, unpicked by the birds and now decomposed to a mulch; the stench of rotting leaves, a reminder that Autumn was well advanced. Predominantly the aroma was that of badger, an earthy odour which spoke of clean animals, wafting out of the deep holes, and from somewhere close by the strong stench of the animals' toilet, for this creature never fouled its living quarters.

Faint sounds which they attempted to identify; swift scurryings amongst the layer of leaves, mice and voles searching for fallen beechmast, hurrying to feed and return to their holes in case there was an owl abroad. Slower, less stealthy movements, a hedgehog looking for those mice and voles and if his hunt should prove futile then he would resort to worms or nuts. A faint grunt that might have been surprise, then silence. He had smelled the foxes, rolled himself into a protective ball. Rus, for only Rus prowled here, would sniff at him but the dog fox would not attempt to probe those spines. He had learned his lesson long ago when he was a cub.

Rak was nervous, hesitant. Had there been a refuse tip amidst these trees then he would have cast his caution aside, delved amongst the waste in search of something edible. But here there were neither dustbins nor council tips. Just rabbits.

The foxes found the briars, nosed beneath the mesh of entwined thorns. Something in the midst of the thick bushes darted and was gone; the rabbit that had emerged from below to feed had favoured caution. Rus often came to the warren but he did not linger long for his territory was vast and there were always rabbits to be caught on the edge of the sheep fields. Digging for rabbits was time consuming and hard work.

Tika found the first hole, stepped in it and almost lost his balance. Rak joined him and they sniffed together. The smell of rabbits was very strong. They would dig right here.

The excavation of a rabbit hole was far from easy. The briars restricted the foxes, by working together they got in each other's way. Tika only stood back when commanded by Rak, and after a while the older fox rebuked him for laziness. Between them they scratched out a pile of soil, scattered it in all directions. Then the exposed hole dropped almost vertically and that made digging even more difficult; the soil was powdery now, showered down to the next bend and was difficult to scrape away.

Much later, when the clouds had cleared and the stars cast a wan light, Rak and Tika were standing in a hole as deep as their shoulders. Frustration and hunger drove them on, the narrow tunnel was sloping upwards again; once again digging was easier.

Surely they had to reach the far end of the burrow soon, a kind of chamber like the one in the badger sett only much smaller. Here, terrified rabbits would be huddling. Fox jaws would snap, a rabbit apiece and Rak and Tika would feed ravenously, their efforts rewarded.

The burrow was heading for the surface. Had they explored before commencing work then they might have saved themselves a laborious task, dug down and cut off their prey's retreat. Rak supposed that rabbits skulked in terror when danger threatened; the entrances were too small for either foxes or terriers to go below ground and flush them out. All this was new but they would learn.

Suddenly the remainder of the burrow avalanched into the hole in which the foxes stood. Soil showered down, roots of undergrowth came with it. It was sometime before Rak understood and by then he had not the energy to try to explain to his companion. The burrow was merely a single channel, a hole at both ends. A daytime bolt-hole in which a rabbit rested. If a stoat or weasel found an entrance, the rabbit fled out of the other end.

Which, in all probability, the rabbit they had disturbed earlier had done. Whilst they were digging from one end, it had long ago escaped out of the other.

The foxes were hungrier than ever.

Dawn found Rak and Tika on the edge of the sheep fields. They had wandered on, always alert for the prowling Rus. Somewhere, far away, they had heard the screeching of a vixen; had he not been so tired and hungry then Rak might have answered her calling for the urge within him might have been stronger.

After a time she fell silent. Rak hoped that it was Rus

53

who had gone to her so that his thoughts would not be on trespassing rivals for the moment.

The morning dawned misty; a fog that hung on the hilltops enshrouded them in a grey vapour, the time of day and the season when rotting blackberries smelled strongest and cobwebs draped every bush. A carrion crow cawed, glided off downhill. Woodpigeons clattered out of their roosts, flighted off to breakfast on dew-drenched clover. The kind of morning which never happened on a city railway embankment.

The sheep were still huddled in a corner of the field, nervous because the mist might cloak unseen danger – a stray dog from the village below. All except one, a ewe that lay on its back twenty yards from the hedgerow, all four legs pointing skywards. A cast sheep, one that had fallen and rolled during the night hours and had not been able to regain its balance. It had died before morning.

Rak and Tika approached it warily, circled it several times before they were satisfied that it was dead. Sheep were even larger animals than badgers and the foxes were still uncertain of the temperament of that species.

Now they sniffed it, the odour of the flesh was reminiscent of some of those tasty meat scraps which they had devoured greedily from city dustbins. Rak scratched at the fluffy coat, it was very thick. There was meat beneath it and he was starving, he couldn't wait.

Never in his life before had he launched such a frenzied attack with his teeth, his jaws ripped, tore out balls of wool; once he almost choked on one that clung in his mouth. Snarling, maddened by hunger, he was joined by Tika. A length of skin ripped, peeled, came away. Now the flesh was bared, red meat that was barely cold, fresher than any they had ever found amidst the city refuse.

They ate, gorged themselves until they were heavy with

their unexpected repast. Only then did they turn away, head back uphill towards the distant wood.

The badgers had already returned to the sett for they were not creatures to linger abroad once day had broken. Rak and Tika entered by the big hole beneath the towering oak, flung themselves down on the floor of the upper gallery. And slept more soundly than they had done since leaving the embankment.

Chapter Seven

When Rak awoke from his exhausted sleep, Tika asked once again when they were going to set out for home. Rak, who would have preferred time to get his bearings, told him they would start out at daybreak on the following day rather than travel by night for the first stage of their journey. That way Rus would surely have returned to his earth from his nocturnal wanderings and they would be well clear of his domain by the time darkness fell again.

Tomorrow they would leave this awful place forever.

Rak and Tika waited for the badgers to return to the sett at daybreak, listened to them going down to the lower gallery. There was a lot of shuffling about, a noise that sounded as if Shaf was quarrelling with one of the other badgers. It must have been a minor dispute because soon all went quiet. Shortly afterwards Rak went to the entrance which descended into the bowels of this underground animal fortress and strained his cocked ears until he heard the occupants begin to snore.

Tika had been impatient throughout, he did not see why

they must await the badgers' homecoming from their nocturnal food foraging before leaving. Rak explained that for various reasons it might be necessary for the foxes to return to this place, in which case it was preferable if their hosts were unaware of their decision to leave. Their departure might be interpreted as ingratitude and the badgers might refuse to allow their guests to resume their tenancy of the upper gallery. As it was, if the foxes chose to return at any time, the badgers would think that they had merely been on an extended hunting trip.

Tika was puzzled, surely they would not be coming back. He, personally, had no wish to spend the entire Winter cohabiting with these surly creatures. But he would go wherever Rak went, he had no wish to be left on his own.

It was broad daylight by the time the two foxes emerged above ground. An overcast sky had them blinking, waiting for their eyesight to adjust. There would be rain before the day was out, already the wind was freshening, there was a moistness in the atmosphere. It wasn't a time to undertake a long journey; Rak might have postponed it until the morrow had it not been for Tika's impatience. If they went back below ground then Tika would only pester again and Rak was in no mood for that.

They needed to eat first, that was imperative because there was no way of knowing when they might next find food. It was better to fill their stomach now whilst they had the opportunity.

That morning, Rak could not get Shi out of his thoughts. His concern was for her whereabouts, what had happened to her. Was she alive or dead? Why had the humans brought the foxes out here? Questions to which he had no answer but he no longer trusted Man. It gave him a sense of abandonment; once he had relied upon Man for his living, now his life depended upon avoiding him. It was both confusing and frightening.

A flock of crows lifted off the remains of the fallen sheep, cawing angrily at being disturbed from their breakfast. They circled, still cawing; swooped and rose again, mobbing the foxes. A harsh chorus, their wingbeats slow and heavy, the corvid abuse shattered the early morning silence.

Tika was scared, he feared lest these black birds might swoop on him, peck at his eyes. He was familiar with the species, there were always a few feeding on the refuse tip back home but those always departed when foxes or dogs appeared. These were fierce, arrogant, would not give up their early morning repast without a fight. They were trying to frighten away the intruders; when that did not work would they attack?

Tika was hungry, he raced on ahead of Rak. If the foxes ate quickly, gorged themselves and then departed, the crows would be able to return to their feast.

Corvids and owls had been feeding on the carcass. Much of the fleece had been torn away, exposing a mulch of blood-ied flesh where hooked beaks had pecked and talons had raked. But there was still meat in plenty and Tika was not waiting for his companion.

The younger fox's greed was his undoing. He bounded forward, stood astride the carrion, and even as his sharp teeth sank into the torn flanks, his hindleg touched against something hard; something metallic. Something which sprang, jumped, fastened on to his foot and sank through fur and flesh, grated on bone.

The excruciating pain brought with it terror; a backward leap, checked by a clanking chain, caught him off balance and threw him, rolled him. The taut chain held him, a tension that went right down to the steel trap with closed jaws and the heavy wooden peg which secured it.

The crows dived low, would maybe have attacked the helpless fox there and then had not Rak greeted them with snapping jaws. The birds lifted to a chorus of corvine insults, wheeled again.

Rak could not understand what had happened to Tika. The other's rear leg was caught in something which bit deeply, already the rusty fur was stained with blood. Rak backed off, he was taking no chances on being the next victim of whatever had caught the writhing Tika.

It was a trap of some kind, even an urban fox could see that, a cruel implement of pain which had lain hidden in the strewn sheep fur, awaiting an unwary victim. Tika was up on three feet, whimpering, straining to free himself. Then he flopped down again, his eyes rolling, pleading with Rak to help him, his mouth starting to froth.

Rak approached warily, fearing lest another steel claw should snap up out of the ground and claim him likewise. Now he was oblivious of the raucous crows whose ragged wingbeats fanned his fur. Tika's body writhed in agony, his desperate pulling was stripping his leg fur from the flesh; the wound was seeping blood.

Rak's jaws closed over the chain, he bit and pulled. His grip threatened to dislodge his teeth, his bite made no impact. He drew back. Tika watched pathetically.

Tika closed his eyes. Then his instinct to survive dominated, he twisted himself round until surely his spine must snap. His own teeth closed over his leg, an inch or so above where the steel ones bit still deeper. If necessary, he would free himself by biting off his own limb.

Rak stared in horror, knew what the other planned to do, a last desperate resort to regain the freedom of a species of the wild. He would help him, bite at the bone, neither of them would rest until the severed foot remained in the trap and Tika was limping away on the other three.

Tika seemed to lapse momentarily into unconsciousness, then revived. His eyes pleaded with Rak to finish the job for him, he no longer had the strength.

The crows had settled at a distance, ghoulish spectators to this mutilation, their only concern the food which was being denied them. Then, suddenly, as one they rose, a black cloud. Their cries were deafening. But now they were neither mobbing nor mocking, their cawing was a cry of alarm.

Rak glanced up and his jaws relaxed their grip on the frayed and chipped bone. He saw the corvids flapping their wings to gain height, seeking safety from the figure which had clambered over a stile in the straggling hedgerow and was walking this way.

Man!

The man was short and stooped, had limbs that fought against arthritic stiffness, a shambling gait. He wore a ragged brown smock and clutched something in his hands. A stick of some kind.

Rak backed off, ran a few yards then stopped and glanced back. The human was hurrying now. Rak bounded again, fifty yards before he checked. Perhaps this man would free Tika. That hope was all that was left to him.

The shepherd paused within a few yards of the trapped fox, a smile on his weatherbeaten features. His lips stretched, he muttered something and raised the stick to his shoulder.

Rak saw Tika jerk; an invisible force rolled the fox caught in the illegal trap, threw him and opened up a gaping wound. Only then did Rak hear the resonant bang, a report which echoed across the surrounding hills like a sudden clap of thunder; a puff of smoke from the end of the stick.

Rak fled blindly, terror-stricken, no thought now for the companion left behind, only for his own safety. A headlong dash, his brush streaming in his wake, his instinct taking him back the way he had come. Because he knew nowhere else in this hostile land, only the deep badger sett where he had been afforded protection. He forgot about Tika. And Shi.

The sticks that went bang and meted out sudden death in human hands had killed. His own life was at risk. Even as he fled, he glanced behind him every few yards, saw that the man was kneeling down, seemed to be examining the inert body of the animal he had trapped.

Rak found himself back in the small wood, in front of him the mound that was the big badger sett, the yawning hole seeming to beckon him. There was safety below ground where Man could not follow, the inhabitants offered him sanctuary if not friendship.

He would not spurn their hospitality this time. He had no intention of venturing beyond Badger Wood in the immediate future.

Chapter Eight

Rak lay in the sett all day, listened to the rhythmic snoring of the badgers below. In his own way he envied them, their existence was much the same as his own had been back in the city; by night they hunted for food, by day they rested. Nobody bothered them, if they had any enemies then those foes did not know of their existence. Life went on the same, day after day, cycles came and went; in the Autumn they mated, they remained snug and warm in the deep gallery during Winter, and in Spring the cubs were born. Nothing changed, year in, year out.

His own lifestyle had been thrown into turmoil. He had only a temporary refuge, in a few months' time he would become an outcast again, a nomad who did not even have a mate for company, for surely these wild, fierce foxes would want nothing to do with him. Far better had he died with Tika, that way all his troubles would have ended.

He heard a movement in the tunnel that led down to the badgers' quarters, a scraping sound, a brushing of stiff fur against hard-packed earth. Rak tensed; seldom did his hosts stir during the daylight hours, their slumber was long and unbroken. Because, unlike himself, they were contented with their lifestyle. Now one of them was coming up here.

A pang of fear, again Rak was the hunted. He backed into a corner, it was too late to flee for the surface because the other was almost in the upper gallery and his retreat was cut off. Perhaps the badger was just restless, or was on his way to their toilet which was to be found in a patch of dense undergrowth down a well-worn track a few yards from the sett. Up until now the badgers had ignored their tenants, it was almost as though they were unaware of their presence. There was no reason why it should be any different now.

Rak watched as the striped head came into view, then the stout body. Small eyes focused on him, held his gaze. This creature was smaller than the rest but he was no cub, one that was destined to be small in stature but none the less powerful for all his lack of size. Rak had glimpsed him before, a young boar who followed in the wake of the others, seemed to keep very much to himself.

There was no hostility in that stare, merely curiosity. The badger squatted, watching the fox, kept his distance as though he was unsure of himself. Rak was suspicious but he was no longer afraid.

Yes, the badger was curious. His name was Ben and he had a story to tell, one that the others in the colony had long tired of hearing. He was in search of a new audience, that much was evident to the fox. And he had come up here whilst the others slept because they would not approve of him associating with a fox. Shaf was insistent that there should be no integration of the species because badgers were superior. Even Rus was regarded by them as being inferior.

There were good and bad humans, Ben began, just as there were good and bad badgers and foxes. And he should know for he had lived amongst them for several seasons.

Ben glanced apprehensively back towards the tunnel, seemed relieved when he heard the steady breathing of slumbering badgers.

In days gone by, Ben said, when they had lived in Hopwas wood, Baal, one of the badgers, had been caught and taken down to a farm in the valley. The farmer there was a rough but kindly man. He had kept Baal as a pet for his children, chained him to a dog kennel in the farmyard. Then Ben had been caught too. With the arrival of a playful badger cub, the children had lost interest in Baal; they forgot to feed him and, unless the farmer remembered, the badger sometimes went hungry. Eventually the farmer had returned the older badger to the wild.

Ben had enjoyed life on the farm. The children had played with him every day after Baal had been released, gave him all sorts of delicacies to eat, titbits which, he confessed, he still yearned for. He opened his jaws, let Rak see gaps where once there had been strong teeth. Ben wasn't old but he had difficulty in eating some of the harder food to be found in the wild, like nuts. Those teeth had just rotted away. He had grown fat at the farm too.

In due course, just as they had lost interest in Baal, the children had tired of Ben. In his gruff kindness, the farmer had set Ben free too.

Because he had once lived amongst humans and been the centre of attention, Shaf resented Ben. In fact – Ben listened again to make sure that the badgers were still snoring – secretly the badger leader hated him.

No wild animal readily accepts another which has lived with Man, Ben explained, eyeing Rak meaningfully. There is always mistrust, the captive creature has learned that life is easier with humans, the only thing of which it is deprived is its freedom and sometimes that is a price worth paying; there is always enough food, sometimes too much, there is no need to hunt, there is warmth and shelter. You don't have to do anything you don't want to do. But as well as surrendering your freedom to roam at will, your natural instincts are dulled, you lose that sense of alertness upon which you depended in the wild. There was a sadness in Ben's expression, the way he hunched his broad shoulders, hung his striped head. That was how it was with him, even though he had been returned to his native environment. He would never be able to retrieve that which was lost.

After his release it was a long time before he was fit again. But he would never really return to his former fitness. The other badgers in the colony regarded him as soft, a weakling; sometimes some of the young boars bullied him, drove him out of the sett. Which was why he spent days, weeks even, alone up here in the top gallery. But he could not do that if it was occupied by foxes; Ben didn't mind foxes but the other members of the colony would banish him from their midst if he was seen to be cohabiting with another species. Even now he risked their wrath by talking to Rak but when one became very lonely it was necessary to find a companion. An acquaintance, actually, for their association must be a distant one.

All this was the price you paid for living in a human environment, Ben sighed. If he had had his way, he would have stayed there. So would Baal, in fact the older badger was reluctant to go when he was offered his freedom; the farmer had to drive him away with a stick. An animal was either domesticated or wild, it was impossible to enjoy the benefits of both existences.

Rak went on to relate his own life story. There was amazement in those tiny eyes, almost disbelief, as Ben listened. Even one who had lived amongst humans could not envisage an area of scrubland in the heart of a concrete landscape where foxes existed quite happily. Surely any creature of the wild would be glad to leave such a place. No, on reflection, they wouldn't, he decided. Because they would have no idea how to survive; they had never had to hunt for their living. Also, they would not envisage Man as a predator, one who hunted them with dogs, killed them with those sticks that banged instant death. Only when it was too late would they accept that Man's hand was against them. Tika had paid the penalty; Rak must learn from his companion's fatal trust.

Ben shook his head slowly from side to side when Rak mentioned that he and Tika had been starting out on the long journey in quest of their former homeland. As far as Ben knew there were no large human habitations within a long way of here; wherever the city was, it must be far away. Too far for foxes or badgers to travel. Yes, he had heard of foxes being transported out into these parts before, frightened creatures who seemed strangely innocent of the perils of the countryside and who had no idea of how to hunt for food. Most of them perished; one morning, during the course of a hunt, the hounds had killed three with ease, the poor foxes too terrified even to run. On another occasion the men who came with the banging sticks, and used dogs to drive the foxes out of the thick woods to where they waited, shot five. All of them foxes who had no fear of Man, and virtually ran towards the waiting shooters as if they thought that the humans would save them from the dogs. Another one got caught in a shepherd's trap, the kind which Rak had described as having caught Tika.

No, if Rak took Ben's advice, he would think again about leaving the safety of these wooded hills. Man's hand would be against him all the way. And, Ben smiled smugly as a really clever thought occurred to him suddenly, what guarantee did Rak have that if he found his way home he wouldn't be caught up again and brought back here? His best course was to remain where he was, he had the use of the upper gallery in the badger sett for the Winter, and once Spring arrived then there were one or two abandoned fox earths in the fir forest, Ben knew of at least a couple. The best thing Rak could do right now was to find himself a mate and . . .

There was no disguising the sadness, the hunched body, the way the last glimmer of hope faded in the fox's eyes. Was something the matter?

Rak told the badger about Shi, how he would even give up all chance of returning to the embankment just to have her back. Ben had spoken of urban foxes that had been killed by the hounds, shot, trapped . . .

Maybe Shi, like Rak himself, had survived, Ben was quick to offer a ray of hope that was far from convincing. By the law of averages, the odd town fox would live. Well, Rak had, hadn't he? Maybe Shi was hiding somewhere in the hills but the area was so vast that it might take months, even a year, to find her. But, and again Ben thought how clever his suggestion was, all vixens screamed for a mate at this time of the year. If you listened at night you could hear them screeching from far and wide. Now, why didn't Rak go in answer to those cries, be prepared to travel the length and breadth of the hills? If Shi was still alive then she would surely be calling soon. He might just find her.

Ben said that he had better be going; if any of the other badgers chanced to wake and discovered that he had been talking to a fox, he would be in trouble. One last word of warning, though. Ben paused in the entrance to the tunnel. If Rak should take his advice and answer the calling of the vixens, then beware Rus – for the old dog fox could be a terrible adversary if he met with a rival during the mating season.

Chapter Nine

*R*ak watched the badgers leaving the sett, a shambling single file that followed Shaf across the upper gallery and into the exit tunnel which led up to the surface. He noted that Ben brought up the rear, kept his distance as if he sensed that his presence was tolerated rather than welcomed. In a way, Ben was almost regarded as a traitor; they did not trust him.

Rak waited, bided his time. There was no hurry. Often it was well into the night hours before the vixen began calling.

In due course Rak moved out of the sett. The night was still and cloudless, there was a crispness in the air that heralded the first frost of Autumn. The stars offered enough light for a sharp-eyed creature to see by. He stood and smelled the air, scented badger and rabbit, hedgehog and vole. But tonight there was no smell of fox. No Rus. And for that he was grateful.

He headed back into the adjoining fir forest, away from the pastureland, for he had no wish to discover what had become of Tika, whether his companion's shot-blasted body still lay there with a mutilated leg caught in the steel trap.

That shepherd might be lying close by in ambush, awaiting the return of the fox which had escaped him.

The forest was dark with patches of starlight filtering down in places where the overhead branches did not meet. Rak moved stealthily, the thick carpet of pine needles enabling him to walk soundlessly. He stopped, waited; moved on again.

Tonight it seemed as if this alien landscape was deserted or, if not, then the inhabitants hid in their holes and burrows, fearful of whatever stalked these woods. He was afraid, for already he had witnessed cruelty and death on a scale which he had never believed existed. His every step was hesitant, each patch of shadow might hide some diabolical trap set in anticipation of his coming.

Suddenly, a vixen screamed and Rak sprang back, startled. The female of his own species could have been no more than three or four yards from where he crouched. He stared into the blackness, heard a movement, a soft tread. Then her scent wafted to him. She knew he was there, she was waiting for him to go to her, it mattered not to her who he was so long as he was male.

Rak approached cautiously. He saw a shape that was blacker than the enshrouding shadows, a lean creature that flicked its bushy tail from side to side, a pair of eyes that glowed in the darkness, urging him to come closer. Jaws agape, panting.

The vixen was becoming impatient, never before had she had a dog fox keep her waiting. She hissed.

Rak halted. This was not Shi, the shape was wrong, the other was too big and, anyway, Shi would have been familiar with his scent. This was some wild vixen who cared not whether her mate was Rak, the city fox, or . . .

She obviously did care. The eager hiss turned to a warning, stopped him. Her eyes regarded him steadily; there was both disappointment and contempt in them. Who was this male whose coat was in such poor condition, who hung back when a female commanded him to come to her? Some cringing cur akin to the village mongrels which roamed the pasturelands? Who was he?

Rak told her, explained that he was searching for Shi who had once been his mate in a faraway place. His reply was greeted with a snarl that exposed vicious teeth, a warning not to come closer. Her frustration turned to contempt. He was not worthy of being her mate, a weakling who had spent his life in the midst of a human habitat. Begone, scrawny creature, and find the one whom you call Shi. You deserve her as much as she deserves you!

The vixen snapped a warning, watched Rak's every move as he skirted her. A lunge, a feint, just to ensure that he continued on his way. She wanted one who was worthy of her. Where was the mighty Rus tonight?

Rak was glad to be clear of the ill-tempered she-fox. At this time of the year he might have been tempted to linger but he hurried on.

He was barely a hundred yards down the winding track before he heard another vixen scream, one that lingered in the night air, vibrated the stillness. It came from a long way away, perhaps half a mile or more. There was no way of telling whether it was Shi, he had never heard her call before in the Autumn. Back in the city she had no need to because he was always close at hand.

Neither was this vixen Shi. Rak saw her standing on top of a mound and made a detour because he had no wish to be insulted a second time. Even as he skirted her, a third fox was calling, her screams almost pitiful in their desperation for an answering bark.

Rak checked to ensure that his sense of direction was right, sometimes echoes on a still night could be misleading. He heard this vixen begin to call again, knew that she was up in the far reaches of the spruce plantation, just below the skyline. A vantage point, possibly, from where she could survey the patch of open ground below her, glimpse any dog fox who came in search of her.

Some inner sense told Rak that this one, too, would not be Shi but he had to check because he could not be sure. Only when he knew that his mate was not in these hills would he abandon all hope. Then he would make a decision on his future.

He trotted across the tract of treeless ground, headed towards the rise. He knew that the vixen was amongst the scrub; she had spotted him, she did not need to call again, she would wait for him to come to her. The frosty air was thick with her smell, she needed him badly.

Tosca lay in the midst of a pile of dead branches, tree brashings which the forestry workers had piled on this mound two summers ago and had never removed; it gave her both warmth and cover. Above all, she could see without being seen.

She had presumed that it was Rus who had answered her call; but her keen nose told her that it was not her mate of many seasons. She was surprised but she did not mind. She envisaged a fox of the year, an early Spring cub which had grown to maturity, a creature much younger and stronger than herself. But the scent wasn't right, she did not quite know how or why and that confused her. All the same, she would wait, see without being seen. If the other was not to her liking then she would snap at it, and drive it off. Then she would await Rus's arrival. But for the first time over the years that prospect did not excite her as it once had.

Tosca saw the approaching fox as it emerged from some fir saplings and hesitated on the open ground. She noted its nervousness, how its coat was unkempt as though it had not fed properly, and yet it was big and strong. There was an innocence about the way it glanced around; it would have been easy prey for a human lying in wait for it. Or it would have walked into a snare or trap without even suspecting the danger until it was too late. Doubtless it was another of those foxes that had been brought out here from Man's domain, like the dead vixen which Tosca had seen lying on the road on the other side of the village last night. The creature had been so used to vehicles in its former habitat that it had not bothered to get off the road at the sound of an approaching car. The driver might even have run it down deliberately; Man's hand was always against the foxes, he killed them whenever he could.

Tosca felt a pang of pity for this strange dog fox. Her contempt for a lesser specimen of her own species was only temporary, passed as quickly as it had come. Down there was a strong young fox, who had heard her calling and had come in answer. Rus was doubtless seeking out younger vixens right now; his fidelity was questionable. That hurt and angered her, she was lonely, abandoned because she was getting on in years.

Rak saw with disappointment that the vixen who had called was not Shi. He was not surprised, perhaps the next one would be. Or the one after that. He did not even notice this female's ageing, how she walked wearily when she emerged from the brushwood. But she greeted him, she did not spurn him. And that counted for a lot.

She snapped at him but it was only game playing. She pretended to rebuff him but it was a token gesture. Then she stood and waited patiently. She was good for one more litter; the coming Spring would doubtless be her last. She might move away and live in solitude when her cubs were grown up and gone. Or she might die.

Some time later, as she lay beside him in a patch of dying

bracken, Tosca asked him about himself. Again he told the long story, culminating with Tika's killing, and naively he asked if by any chance she had met with a vixen called Shi.

Tosca replied that she had not, surely it would not be the vixen which had been lying dead on the roadside beyond the village; there were innumerable females about here, and one such as his former mate, coming from the city, would be wise to the perils of traffic.

Rak fell silent, a nagging fear spoiling everything that had happened since he had chanced upon this sympathetic vixen. Apart from the badgers' impartial hospitality, no creature in this strange land had actually shown kindness towards him. All the same, he was concerned because there was a dead fox lying by the roadside in the valley.

The stars were fading when he finally rose and left Tosca's side. There was not so much as a farewell between them; Rak did not even notice that she watched him until he was out of sight. Once clear of the fir wood, he broke into a swift canter. He had no thoughts of returning. Foxes met and passed on, never saw each other again. It was often the way of the wild.

Rak's heart was beating fast, his tongue lolled from his mouth as he ran. Across the lower pastures, it never occurred to him to glance upwards to see what had become of Tika. Tika was momentarily forgotten.

Only Shi mattered.

He reached the village, paused. A dilemma, right or left? There was no way of knowing. A milk delivery van clinked to a halt down the road, the driver leaped out, left the engine running. He turned, pointed, shouted something. Rak bounded away in the opposite direction. His choice had been made for him.

Dawn was coming fast, here and there windows were lit

up, farm and forestry workers preparing for a new day. A prowling cat arched its back, stared after the passing fox.

Rak ran on, nose to the ground: scents were familiar from his background, spilled oil and diesel. A hedgehog had been squashed flat by a passing car, he barely gave the crimson and grey morass a second glance.

A sheet of paper wafted in the breeze, might have become airborne had it not been for the soggy mass of cold chips that weighted it on the tarmac. Rak would have paused to scavenge in any other situation but right now he had to find what Tosca had told him about.

Further on, maybe a quarter of a mile beyond the main street, he found what he was looking for. Almost, anyway. There was no vulpine corpse lying ignominiously alongside the verge, it had probably been picked up by one of the hunters who killed their prey with guns; a pelt, when stretched and dried, would fetch a few pounds. Left on the road was a patch of dried blood with some hairs adhering to it.

Rak smelled them but he was not sure enough to identify them positively. Certainly they were from a vixen's coat. That was maybe all he would ever know. Perhaps it was best that way.

He left the village before full daylight, took a circuitous route back up to the hills to avoid the field in which Tika had died. Death, in any form, was something which he could no longer face.

He did not travel all the way back to Badger Wood, instead he lay up in the depths of the fir forest.

His thoughts switched from Shi to something more positive, more tangible. At his lowest ebb he needed a sympathetic protector.

But an urban fox knew that he must wait until Tosca

called before he went to her. An acceptance was dependent upon an invitation.

Tosca was all that was left to him.

Chapter Ten

*T*osca called and Rak went to her.

It was as though she had known all along that he would return, as if she had lain in that pile of brushwood ever since he had left. Because Shi, the vixen from the inner city railway embankment, had most likely been killed on the road and therefore Rak had none other to turn to.

They lay together in the bracken, snug from the cold night air, and Tosca told Rak about herself. She remembered the days when she and Rus had lived down in Hopwas Wood on the lower reaches of this hillside. Those had been days of plenty when Jenkins, the ageing gamekeeper, had reared pheasants for the men who came from the city to shoot. Jenkins set snares to catch the foxes but if you were careful you did not run into one. On moonlight nights the wire nooses glinted so that they could be seen, but on dark nights it was best to hunt well away from the game preserves. A cunning fox learned from the mistakes of his fellow creatures, just as Rak must learn from Tika's.

It was after Jenkins died that Rus had decided that he and Tosca must move up into the hills. For that was when the cruel new gamekeeper, Reuben, took over control of the wood; neither fox nor badger was safe, and in addition to snares he used steel traps with teeth like the one the shepherd had set by the dead ewe which had caught Tika.

From here on the story was only too familiar to Rak, he had heard it all from Ben. The foxes continued to raid the game preserves of Hopwas Wood, but they deserted the traditional earth for nothing was safe there. Now Rus and Tosca were neighbours of the badger colony in Badger Wood, occasionally using that same upper gallery for sanctuary when either the Hunt or the farmers and shepherds with their guns and dogs were in the vicinity. It was a good place; Tosca had no wish to move elsewhere. Surely Rak would want to stay here, too. There was a kind of longing in her eyes, a pleading with him to stay.

Rak fell silent. Was there any reason for him to try to return to the city? Shi was dead, he was sure of that. Maybe there were no foxes left on the embankment, they had all been caught up and transported to remote places. He could find himself alone there; perhaps all the other species had gone, too.

He felt Tosca tense, her head went up, her ears were erect. The night wind rustled the last of the dead leaves which still clung stubbornly to their boughs. Or was it a movement out there, on the fringe of the fir forest, that had alerted her? One of the badgers, possibly.

She was uneasy, restless. Rak heard the sound again, it wasn't just the wind. A low branch sprung back, a dead twig cracked.

And then he saw the fox, a huge creature that seemed to materialize out of the shadows like some spectral being. Its jaws were wide, there was hostility in its eyes and in its very posture, as it scanned the mound in front of it, its gaze coming to rest on that clump of dying bracken.

77

Rus had come for Tosca, to claim her for his own.

Rak trembled; his instinct was to flee but he doubted whether his shaking legs would have had the speed and stamina to outrun his nemesis. Tosca had moved back, the female of the species had no part in this, the law of the wild, of Nature herself. Whatever the outcome of this encounter, she would accept it.

Rak moved out of the undergrowth, began to descend the slope; not because Rus called him, challenged him, but because there was no alternative left to him. Rus stood there motionless, watching, fury and hatred for a lesser rival seething within him.

So, it was the fox who had come from amongst humans who had dared to try to steal his mate, a mangy specimen who did not even know how to hunt! An inferior being, a coward who trembled visibly. Had Rak not been warned to stay away from the vixens in Rus's territory? Had he not been ordered to make himself scarce, to live with the badgers or to leave these hills? Rak's foolishness was unbelievable. Did he really think that he could make a challenge for Tosca who had borne Rus a litter of cubs each Spring for as long as the old fox could remember? Rus prided himself in his offspring, fierce and cunning foxes who would outwit Man, and now this usurper sought to adulterate the regal strain with inferior genes. Rus did not blame Tosca; a vixen called, waited for a mate to come to her. It was Nature's way. But a dog fox made her his own by fighting off all who sought to undermine his supremacy.

Thus it had been for season after season, many a fox had been put to flight by the much feared Rus, had left these hills and never been seen again. Or crawled away to die a lingering death from his wounds!

The sudden lunge caught Rak by surprise. One second Rus was standing there, the next he was airborne, a hurtling bundle of rage and bloodlust, open jaws closing viciously on Rak's shoulder. The force of the attack sent both foxes rolling, snarling and biting.

Somehow Rak loosened the grip on his shoulder, twisted and sprang free. Rus was strong but there was a suppleness lacking in those ageing limbs. He was just a little slower than he had been last mating season when he had vanquished Poul, the almost black fox, and an awful lot slower than a few seasons ago. That was where Rak sensed an advantage; in the meantime he had to keep clear of those teeth. They were as sharp and powerful as they had always been.

Rus crouched, made as if to spring at his adversary, changed his mind. A feint and then he darted in low, snapping for the flanks. Rak jumped, came down on the other side of him. He snapped and felt his teeth close on flesh, then he was out of reach again.

Rak's shoulder hurt, he knew it was bleeding but he could not afford to lose his concentration. They were circling, snarling jaws keeping each other at bay. A game of waiting; you looked for a weakness and seized upon it. But for the moment there were no weaknesses, no lapses in defensive tactics.

Rak leaped back, dropped into shadow; his opponent could not see him clearly now. Rus hesitated, he was too wise, too experienced a fighter to rush in blind. He just stood there; Rak had to come out some time or else go away and concede the contest.

Rak rushed, twisted his body to the right and left, attacked from the right. Another sharp bite, his clamped teeth came away with a tuft of hair. Rus hissed, that bite had hurt him. He retaliated quickly, marked an ear and almost paid the price as those teeth closed within an inch of his throat.

The two foxes went back to circling each other, maybe hoping to wear the other down. For Rus, time was not on his side, he must bring this to a conclusion quickly. His stamina was not what it once had been.

Tosca crossed Rak's mind; just in time he stopped himself from turning his head to look for her. There would be time enough for that afterwards; in the meantime he could risk no distractions.

The pace had slowed, Rak was tiring and he knew that his opponent must be also. They crouched, snarled, but neither launched another attack. Backing off, stalking each other, neither ventured within reach of their enemy.

Then Rak leaped; they met, standing at full stretch on their hindlegs, teeth countered teeth, held in a jaw-lock, mouths frothing. They parted, kept their distance again.

Tosca watched from the foot of the slope, her keen eyes flicking from one to the other, her expression impassive. Perhaps she was impartial; only the victor would be her mate for vixens did not accept a loser – Rus, whom she had known for many seasons, or Rak, the stranger from a strange land? Whichever way the battle went, she would not spurn her suitor.

Both foxes appeared to be dragging themselves around now, their feet scratching circular furrows in the ground, both bore bare patches where hair had been ripped from their coats. Both were bloodied.

The sky was lighter, a hint of dawn. The shadows melted, there was no place left to hide momentarily in an attempt to lure the other to make a false move. This contest could not last much longer.

Rus rushed headlong and that was his undoing. Perhaps he sensed that his strength was ebbing, that he could only muster one last effort. Or maybe he had over-estimated his opponent's tiredness. Whichever, he was neither fast nor strong enough. One moment Rak was there for the taking, the next he had corkscrewed his battered body, dodged the charge and taken Rus from behind.

Grimly, using every ounce of his waning strength, Rak bore Rus to the ground, straddled his back and clamped him in the neck. The latter hissed, his eyes bulged and he bubbled saliva. He braced himself, tried to jerk upwards to throw off his aggressor but Rak held on. Slowly, surely, those teeth dug deeper, secured a stranglehold; one downward pressure and the neck would snap. The vertebra was old and brittle.

But Rak held back. Not out of mercy, simply that he had never killed before, not even a rabbit. He saw no reason to now for there was no way that Rus was going to return to the fray.

Finally, Rak loosed his hold, felt the other go limp beneath him; Rus was still breathing, his eyes opened, he looked up. His expression was one of puzzlement. Why had Rak not killed him? The loser of such a contest either fled ignominiously or died, there was no compromise. But here he was, lying there at the mercy of his conqueror and Rak was simply standing there watching him. Was it some cruel game, just when he thought he was going to be allowed to live, he would be killed?

But, no. Rak turned his back, left him there. You are defeated, Rus, no longer is this your kingdom. Begone, find somewhere far from here to eke out your final years, live in solitude, an outcast.

Rus struggled to his feet. He did not glance round for he had no wish to meet Tosca's contemptuous stare. He had served her well, his regret was that he was not able to father her last litter; that his defeat had not been at the jaws of some noble hill fox instead of a scraggy animal from an urban area who was used to soft living. But fate had decreed it so. The other was strong in spite of his former scavenging lifestyle, he had survived where many of his colleagues had perished. In that respect, Rus admired him.

Battered, bleeding from a deep bite, Rus staggered away, determined that he was going to make it over the first rise, where he would be hidden from their view before he flopped down to rest. Then, he would travel in easy stages to some place far from here where the fox population had never heard of Rus. He would be just another fox and the others would not bother him.

Rak turned, saw that Tosca was watching him. There was admiration in her soft eyes, sympathy for one who had not escaped unscathed. And a lot more that was beyond his comprehension.

He staggered across to join her and together they headed for the safety of the fir forest and a new beginning.

Chapter Eleven

Rak was surprised to find the large fox earth in such close proximity to Badger Wood. During those few nocturnal forays from the sett, he had never even suspected its presence; he had walked within yards of it.

Now he followed on the heels of Tosca, down narrow tracks that wound back on themselves, virtually dragging himself in her wake.

The earth was situated just beyond the eastern fringe of the age-old wood, the prevailing winds taking the scent of fox away in the opposite direction which was probably why he had overlooked it. The brambles that grew above it acted as a perfect screen, thick and thorny, denser even than those beneath which the rabbit warren lay.

The interior was roomy, there was more than enough space in which to rear the largest litter which Tosca might expect next Spring. It was old, too, maybe even as old as the badger sett. Doubtless it had been enlarged and renovated over the years. It was a fitting lair, indeed, for a fox who had borne such a reputation as Rus.

But now Rus was gone, he would never return, and this

was the home of Rak, the urban fox who had known only a scratched out earth in an overgrown railway embankment in the heart of an inner city.

Rak and Tosca lay down together in the cool darkness. Soon her rough tongue was seeking out his wounds, licking them with a tenderness that soothed their smarting.

He was exhausted; he gave up the fight to remain awake, and even whilst he slept he was aware that she continued to caress him. For now he was her mate, he had overcome the mighty but ageing Rus in combat and had earned that right. No fox could take that away from him this season.

When he awoke, aching but refreshed, he sensed that it was night again by the crisp coldness in the atmosphere. For a moment he feared that everything might have been a dream, that there would be no Tosca by his side. But Tosca was there, watching over him. He wondered if she had slept, more likely she had just dozed.

He was stiff when he stood up, but much of the soreness in his wounds had gone. Tosca moved towards the exit, looked back. They were going out, that much was obvious. They were hungry, they had to find food. Rak was worried in case she planned to go down to the sheep fields where that dead ewe lay with a trap set close to it, and the shepherd was waiting close by to blast whatever it caught. But, to Rak's relief, Tosca sniffed into the wind, and headed in the opposite direction.

There were more fields up here but much rougher than the closely grazed pastureland; a moor that had been sold off a few years previously to the shepherds and they had divided it up with barbed wire fencing. The foxes easily squeezed beneath the bottom strand. The grass was coarser, spikey tufts, patches of gorse that spread each year until eventually they would cover the uneven ground. In places the ground was boggy, animal tracks skirted the marshy areas, they knew this terrain better than Man had ever done.

Tosca was familiar with this territory, she had often accompanied Rus here when first they had moved from Hopwas Wood. There was a deep pool in the centre, almost hidden by dense reeds and its surface was covered with algae during the summer. She remembered seeing a dead sheep floating in it once. She always kept well clear of it.

She dropped behind Rak, reminded him that it was his job to hunt, because when she had a litter in the Spring he would need to supply food for the cubs. He had to be an expert at catching rabbits because then they would need a regular supply.

Rak was nervous, he sensed that she was putting him to the test. He had only once caught a rabbit in his life and then he had let it go. Perhaps it wasn't as difficult as he anticipated; you stalked them whilst they were grazing out on open ground; you had to be fast enough to intercept them before they darted into cover. Catching them should not be too hard, it was sure to be a lot easier than digging out a warren! He was too ashamed to tell Tosca about how he and Tika had scratched out that burrow and found it was only a bolt hole. He would not mind killing a rabbit; he supposed that you just gripped it in your jaws and bit hard. Anyway, he would soon find out.

Tosca stopped on the top of a rise. Rak glanced back and it was obvious that she did not intend to follow him any further. She was going to stay right there; from this elevated position she could see over most of the moorland. It was a good vantage point; from now on she was just a spectator. Go and show me how you catch rabbits, Rak – because Rus was the best there was at hunting, no fox could better him. Not just rabbits either, he could infiltrate a gamekeeper's preserves, take a pheasant and bring it home, unerringly dodging all the traps and snares that had been set for him.

Rus had been a fine mate. She missed him but she could not dispute the law of the wild. Every vixen had to accept the challenge of a rival during the mating season. Whether or not you kept your mate depended upon the outcome. At least Rus was alive; often an older dog was killed in the battle for supremacy. But he would not be returning, and if he did then she would drive him away. No female wanted a loser. The prospect of a much younger mate was an exciting one. She was sure that Rak was quick and strong, he had needed to be to defeat an experienced victor of so many encounters like Rus. Rak would almost certainly be a good hunter, too.

Rak was not a good hunter.

Tosca watched him in amazement. There were some rabbits feeding out beyond the nearest patch of gorse, her keen eyes picked them out in the faint starlight, dark blobs that were visible against the frosted grass. Instinctively her sharp nose checked for wind direction; the faint breeze was blowing from her to the gorse. Had she been much closer, then the rabbits would either have scented her or else heard her stealthy tread on the crisp ground. Any hunting beast would have known that it was necessary to make a wide detour and approach its prey with the wind blowing in his face.

Rak, apparently, was quite ignorant of this basic technique.

He was making directly for the rabbits. At least he used every scrap of cover, crept from tussock to tussock, used the shadow of the gorse to his advantage. That much was in his favour but it was not sufficient. One of the coneys stopped feeding, sat upright on its haunches. Another followed, then the rest. Every one of them was alert, suspicious. They had heard something that alarmed them.

Tosca stared in disbelief. Rak was still thirty yards from his intended prey; he had not even stopped and crouched. That way the rabbits might have resumed grazing after a while. No, he simply carried on regardless until the rabbits saw him, panicked and bounded for cover.

Rak broke into a sprint, his brush streaming behind him, a futile chase. The last of the rabbits gained the safety of the dense gorse several yards ahead of him. He stopped in dismay, then turned and looked back to where his new mate stood silhouetted on the skyline. His open jaws, his tongue lolling out, was an expression of puzzlement. How on earth had those rabbits known of his presence? Surely, the shadows had hidden him well enough.

Even from that distance he sensed Tosca's disapproval, her obvious contempt for his naïve approach. Slowly, she descended the slope, her head seemed to shake from side to side. She stopped within a yard of him, stood there looking at him. Why on earth had he not used the wind to his advantage? Didn't he know that even the faintest of breezes bore scents and noises?

Tosca was unable to hide her astonishment. She had never heard of a fox who did not know how to hunt rabbits. Well, there was only one thing for it, she would have to teach him. And he had better learn well or else he would not survive in this place. He would starve, and so would she and her cubs next Spring!

They moved on, this time with Tosca in the lead. Rak noted how she stopped every so often, listened and scented; then crept forward again. Until they emerged from a patch of scrub and saw three rabbits feeding unconcernedly out on the tussocky grass.

Tosca ordered her companion to stay where he was, to watch and to learn. This stalk would not be an easy one for the rabbits were on open ground, the only cover was the spikey grass.

He watched her go, saw how she moved, belly to the ground, stopping every so often. She travelled wide of them, a distance of a hundred yards or more before she cut in; now she was directly opposite to where Rak lay.

At times he was unable to see her, caught a brief glimpse and then she was closer. And closer.

A sudden rush; he heard a rabbit squealing pitifully. Two bolted in the direction of the distant gorse; the third struggled in Tosca's jaws. Then the creature was hanging limp and silent and Tosca was trotting back to where Rak watched in admiration.

He stood back as she laid her catch down, held it with her foot whilst she ripped at it with her sharp teeth. She ate it, did not offer him any because she was the tutor and hers was the reward. Now he must show her that he had learned, he must catch his own supper.

Rak had always been quick to learn. There was a single rabbit out in the open. In order to approach it he must travel upwind, move slowly and use every available scrap of cover. He was nervous, he dared not fail with Tosca watching his every move.

Once the rabbit's head went up; a quick look around and then it was lowered again. If it had heard anything, then it was a false alarm. It was hungry, that was all that mattered.

Now Rak was within two yards of it. Its back was towards him. He considered risking a leap. No, he must be sure. He edged a little closer. And that was when the rabbit became aware of his presence.

In one co-ordinated movement it jumped up and ran, ears flat along its head, white tail bobbing as if to taunt its hunter. For a second Rak froze, then his hind legs sprung him into pursuit. There was an urgency which powered him, one that transcended hunger. He was on trial; already he had earned the contempt of his new mate, he must regain her admiration. The defeat of Rus in combat was not enough.

Sheer desperation gave him the speed he needed, he closed the gap between him and his intended prey. Two yards; a yard. The outline of the gorse ahead loomed up, once the fleeing creature gained the safety of those spikey bushes all was lost.

A bounding leap, he should have had the rabbit, grabbed it and held it aloft. Instead it jinked, swerved away so that his teeth snapped together just as they closed. The rabbit turned, darted away at right angles, regained the lead which it had lost. At least it was now heading away from cover, back out on to the moor.

Now the chase was zig-zagging, in and out of tussocks, constantly changing direction. Rak's frustration increased, he was aware how his heart pounded.

And then he lost sight of the rabbit; one second its fluffy tail was bouncing in front of him like a will-o'-the-wisp, the next it had vanished. He skidded to a halt in the soft ground, looked around him in disbelief. Perhaps there was a burrow close by, a bolt-hole that had an entrance and an exit and the fugitive was lying trembling below ground, waiting for him to leave. If he tried to scratch it out, then it would simply run for freedom at the open end. It would have a good start on him, it might well make it to safety.

He was perplexed. He glanced guiltily behind him, could just discern Tosca's outline against a starry background. She was watching his every movement; you've learned how to stalk, Rak, but you let him escape when the kill was there for the taking. *Find him*!

Rak sniffed about, poked his nose into the long grasses. Behind him a startled snipe took to the wing, screeching its alarm call, a *scaarp-scaarp*, jinking and swerving away into the darkness. Further away some more of these long-billed wading birds followed, angry at being disturbed but wary of anything that moved on the moor. Their survival depended upon their alertness.

Suddenly Rak froze into immobility, poised on three legs. He had picked up the rabbit's scent, it was very strong. Yet there was only grass around him, not even thick tufts, an area which the hardy hill sheep had grazed down to the butt. It was boggy, too.

Then, without warning, the missing rabbit jumped up in front of him, it had been lying in a slight hollow, possibly a hare's form, and its grey fur had blended perfectly with the frosted grass.

It might have escaped him had it not been exhausted after the lengthy pursuit, or perhaps it was the waterlogged ground that slowed it down. Whichever, Rak's pounce took him on to it, he pinned it down amidst a splashing and spraying of peaty water. He floundered, panicked for a second but he managed to secure his grip on the wriggling creature, dragged it with him on to firmer terrain. It was then that the rabbit began to squeal, a shrill cry which embodied pain and fear, the knowledge that it was about to die.

Rak almost dropped it; had it not been for Tosca's approach he might have done so. He heard her coming, soft quick footfalls, and then she was standing there looking at him. Her expression was one of mingled relief and praise; it should have been an easy catch right at the start but he had persevered and all was well in the end. That was what mattered. It did not matter how you caught a rabbit, provided you did. That way a vixen and her cubs wouldn't starve.

Now all that was left to Rak was to kill his catch.

Tosca was becoming impatient. The hardest part was done, why was Rak just standing there with the rabbit struggling and screaming? You killed your prey swiftly, not like those domesticated cats that strayed up from the village and played cruel games with mice and young rabbits for hours on end. You caught and you killed, not because you were merciful, simply that you needed food to eat. Sometimes, if you managed to gain entry to a henhouse, you slaughtered wantonly – but that was your nature, the bloodlust ran hotly, got out of control, there was no way you could stop it. Out here in the wild, though, a swift kill was the culmination of a lengthy stalk or a hard chase. Rak must learn to kill, it was the only way to survive.

Kill it, Rak!

Rak killed the rabbit. In his own way he would have preferred to do it instantly, not out of compassion towards his terrified captive but because he wanted to get it over and done with. Tosca was becoming angry at the delay; she seemed to think that Rak was trying to avoid the task, that he lacked expertise and wanted her to do it for him. But she had already demonstrated the *coup-de-grace*, he had witnessed it; now it was up to him. She did not tolerate fools gladly.

Eventually the rabbit was dead. As Tosca had eaten the previous one, she stood and watched her mate devour this latest kill, for there would be no refuse to scavenge in these wooded hills.

When only the furred feet remained, Tosca turned with a swish of her tail. The lessons were finished, now they would set off on a roundabout route which would eventually bring them back to Badger Wood. It was important that Rak became familiar with his terrain for before long he must hunt alone. Long before her cubs were born he must become a proficient hunter.

Where once Rus had ruled, Rak, the urban fox, had come to usurp the kingdom of the wild. Tosca was accustomed to the ways of a fierce ruler and she would settle for nothing less. The name of Rak would soon be feared amongst the other foxes which inhabited these uplands.

Chapter Twelve

Winter waited until after Christmas before venting its icy wrath upon the countryside. Autumn had been dry and sunny with early morning mists and overnight frosts, nights when the creatures of the wooded slopes enjoyed being abroad.

Even the hedgehog stirred from his hibernation in the hole in a bank on the sheltered side of Badger Wood which had once been a wasps' nest; he had enlarged it, lined it with moss and leaves so that it was snug and warm. However, the mild days made him restless and occasionally he ventured forth at night and foraged for beetles on the leafy floor.

He was wary of the badgers for they were not as easily deterred by his sharp spines as were the foxes. But even the humble hedge pig, who mostly minded his own business, could not recall having seen Rus lately. That other fox which he had met once or twice on his travels was a strange one, indeed.

On their first meeting the hedgehog had instinctively curled himself up into a ball at the other's approach. Just to be on the safe side. Usually a fox, whether it was Rus or any of the others who sometimes prowled here, ignored him and went on their way, for they had experienced the sharpness of those prickles in their younger days and had not forgotten. But this fellow had come right up to him, pawed at him in an attempt to roll him over. The dog fox had yelped with pain and fled. It was certainly odd that a fully grown vulpine should have interfered with him, the hedgehog thought. But, for sure, he would not do so again!

Pyne, the nomadic polecat, watched Rak hunting the sheep fields. He had travelled far to these parts from his native mountains many Winters ago and was still searching for a mate but had so far not even encountered another of his own species. Pyne lay full length along the lower branch of a huge oak tree; it was a good point of ambush for one so agile as he, for rabbits frequently travelled below on their way to and from the pasturelands. Rabbits never looked up, they did not see him until it was too late. Right now, though, Pyne's attention was focused on Rak.

That fox was behaving strangely, you only had to watch him to realize that. He seemed to have no idea of quartering as he hunted for coneys hiding in the tussocks. Instead, he travelled a straight course, often retraced his tracks, hunted ground which he had already covered and seemed oblivious of the fact. Frequently rabbits broke cover behind the fox, made it to the safety of the wood with ease.

Nevertheless, Rak did catch rabbits, enough to satisfy the critical Tosca, anyway. Often his lengthy stalks proved abortive. He had learned the importance of wind direction and knew how to make the most of any available cover, but he lacked stealth.

The rabbits which he managed to catch were slow moving, some even sat out in the open and appeared to be unaware of an approaching fox. They squealed briefly before they died.

Pyne could have slaughtered many, if not all, of those

rabbits whose eyes bulged and festered so that they were blinded, and who did not seem able to hear, either. Blind and deaf, they died within a few days of contracting this malady and the crows came and scavenged their carcasses. Pyne, like Sacko the stoat, preferred to hunt the healthy rabbits for he loved the thrill of the chase. There was more to hunting than just killing.

Rak, though, seemed quite happy to pick up these suffering creatures, carried them home proudly to Tosca. She no longer accompanied her mate on his hunting expeditions for she sensed that this time her litter, her last, would be born early. Her maternal instincts urged her to remain below ground. She was ageing, she tired easily, and she slept more than usual.

The snow which came at the end of a frosty week when the ground was hard, deepened and drifted in an overnight blizzard. The gale dropped but it continued to snow steadily for another whole day. Then the frost returned and froze the landscape so that foxes and badgers were able to walk comfortably on top of the drifts, over hedges and fences; even the stream in the dingle froze.

Rak scraped the entrance to the earth clear and pushed his head outside. The snow reflected against the night sky, it was brighter than moonlight. Branches bowed beneath their frozen burden, everywhere was still and silent, it was as though every creature had deserted these hills in search of a warmer habitat. The badgers would already have left the sett; maybe their claws were sharp and powerful enough to dig down through the snow to the carpet of leaves where mice and voles sheltered, or a hibernating hedgehog, whose spines were no defence against its most feared predator.

Tosca had told Rak that the rabbits would be found in the fir forest in such weather conditions. The grass, their regular food supply, would be buried beyond their reach so they would go in search of young saplings, gnaw the succulent bark. There was no undergrowth in the thick plantation where the sunlight never penetrated, no cover for them. Move stealthily, be prepared to lie up for long periods in a suitable place of ambush, and a patient fox was sure to be rewarded with an unwary rabbit.

Tosca declined to accompany him. She felt the cubs inside her, she was maybe only six weeks off giving birth. Her maternal instincts advised her to rest up as much as possible, a long trek would be both unwise and unnecessary; it was Rak's duty to hunt for her, he would surely return with a freshly killed rabbit. All the rabbits he brought her were suffering with disease. They were easy prey even for a town fox but that did not matter, the meat was tasty and satisfied her hunger. And all the time Rak was learning; eventually he would be able to stalk and run down healthy rabbits. It was only a matter of time before he became as proficient as Rus had been.

She no longer yearned for her mate of many seasons. A younger dog was a much more exciting proposition. But next Autumn he might sense that her breeding days were over and go in search of a litter-bearing vixen. If that happened, then she would accept the law of Nature. That was when she would pine for Rus, she might even leave Badger Wood and go in search of him so that they could spend their last days together. In the meantime, though, Rak was her mate. She would not desert him. Once the cubs were able to fend for themselves she would not see much of him throughout the summer months; when the leaves began to fall, she would call for him. He would either return or ignore her. Only then would she know.

Rak did not like the forest; here in a silent world of near-pitch blackness, only patches of snow that had managed to find a way down through the entwining branches half-lit the gloom of small clearings. Nothing moved, not even the badgers had come here, he was wasting his time. He dared not travel too far into the deep woods in case he became lost.

Then, ahead of him, he heard a fast thumping. A rabbit had either heard or scented him, had bolted for safety. Rak lifted his nose but there was no hint of wind, he was at a loss to know in which direction to travel so that his intended prey was oblivious of his presence. Perhaps he might do better on the edge of the wood; rabbits seldom ventured far from their warren.

He remembered the ferny dingle on the south side of the forest, the apex of the grazing fields, a sheltered hollow where the sheep huddled in stormy weather, cosy even to a town fox. Of course, there would be snow lying but it would not have drifted there like it had in the open.

Rak had travelled that way once or twice on his nocturnal hunting. There were always rabbits to be seen on the slopes and the one time he had visited it by day, he had spied a cock pheasant strutting down by the stream, a majestic bird whose red and gold plumage scintillated in the Autumn sunshine. That pheasant was alert to danger; he had spied Rak from a distance and had immediately taken to the wing, gliding down the hillside towards the village, his taunting cry of *cock-up* deliberately mocking the fox. A bird of several seasons, he had long sharp spurs to prove his age. He had survived both predators and Man's gun for too long to allow a scraggy fox like that one to stalk him!

Rak had a retentive memory, a legacy of his urban life, for in the city there was always something different to note; out here, life was routine, an animal kingdom as opposed to Man's domain. Foxes in the wild saw little to remember, one day was much the same as another.

He knew that he didn't have to go across the field where

Tika had been trapped by the ewe's body; there was a much shorter and more sheltered approach which he had used that day when he had fled from the shepherd. There was a fire-break which divided the two large conifer plantations. Where the track began to slope downhill, a narrow animal-run forked to the left; follow this for about a hundred yards and it brought you to the rusted forestry perimeter fence. Here there was a gap beneath the mesh where foxes and badgers had pushed their way through night after night; you just had to squeeze beneath the lower strand and you emerged into the dingle. In all probability the shepherd had not repaired it because there wasn't room for a sheep to get through. Or perhaps he had not even noticed it. Whichever way, it would suit Rak's purpose tonight. He just hoped that it was not buried beneath a deep snowdrift.

It wasn't.

The driving snow had accumulated on the east-facing slopes of the small valley, the western side and the dingle were almost clear, just a powdering of frozen snow where the blizzard had dusted over it. As Rak stood watching from the trees, he saw how the banks of flattened bracken glinted with a spectral hue; how the bottom through which the frozen stream ran was in pitch darkness. He could not see that break in the fence but he would find it all right. And doubtless there would be rabbits feeding on the open grass and heather. He thought he could hear their pulling and munching but it might have been the sheep further afield. He had learned that sheep were a valuable aid to a stalk, for a fox could move amongst them almost unnoticed. Sheep seldom took any notice of foxes.

Rak moved forward, and walked along the bank of the stream. The water was frozen solid, it would have borne his weight but the ice might have crackled and warned the rabbits of his approach. An icy gust of wind ruffled his ears; for once the elements were with him, he would be neither scented nor heard.

He found the gap under the fence by following the mesh along until he came to that place where the netting was pushed outwards. He dropped on to his stomach and began to ease his body beneath it.

And that was when something slid over his head, and tightened around his neck.

Rak drew back, almost choked. He stopped; whatever was cutting through his fur and into his flesh, checked. He fought for breath and for a few seconds his world went blacker than the night around him.

His first thought was that he had pushed his neck into a square of sheep netting; in which case all he had to do was to gently wriggle it free. He moved his head from side to side, but whenever he pushed or pulled the constriction came with him.

It was too dark to see what it was that held him; all he knew was that it was a length of strong wire that had somehow slipped over his head and encircled his neck. If he went backwards or forwards, it threatened to strangle him. If he lay motionless beneath the fence it merely held him. No amount of shaking his head could dislodge it.

Once he panicked, almost throttled himself when the length of steel wire that ran through the eyelet hooked over a broken strand of fence. Luckily, it came free. By this time he had learned that if he lay motionless it did not hurt.

But, there was no disputing the fact that he was anchored firmly to the fence. There was no escape, he was trapped.

He remembered Tika in that cruel trap. The young dog fox had been caught by the leg, and Rak had tried to bite off the other's limb in order to free him. Had the man with the stick that banged instant death not suddenly appeared, then Tika might be alive today even though he would have been a cripple. Rak attempted to twist his head round, seeking a teeth-hold on the wire, wondered if he might be able to chew through it. But he only succeeded in tightening the noose; he had to stop and gasp for breath. The wire was tantalisingly beyond the reach of his jaws.

He found himself peering into the darkness of the dingle, tensing when he heard a movement in case it was that shepherd coming to blast his trapped body. But it was only a sheep, a stupid creature that continued with its frosted grazing, ignoring Rak's struggles. It might not even have noticed his plight.

Rak knew without any doubt that this was yet another human device set to trap an unwary fox. Had not Ben, or was it Shaf, told him how the humans in these hills waged an unending war against foxes. Even at the height of his terror, Rak found himself pining for the distant city where people put out food scraps for the fox population, and no hand was lifted against the nocturnal predators. He should not have lingered here, he should have ignored the badgers' hospitality and left Tosca to find a mate of the wild, obeyed his instincts and set off for home. He would surely have found the railway embankment again after all this time.

Was this the fate that had befallen Shi or had she been killed on the road outside the village? Certainly she was dead, he now had no doubt about that. Far better that it had been beneath the wheels of a fast travelling vehicle than this slow, agonizing death by strangulation.

Man would come at daylight, Rak was sure. He glanced skywards but the stars still twinkled brightly in a velvet sky. He had lost all conception of time, he had no idea how much longer he had left to live.

He barked, a sharp yap of hopelessness that hung in the still, icy atmosphere. He had no idea why he gave voice, it was certainly not the call that he would have used to answer a vixen's scream. If it was a cry for help, then it was futile for no prowling fox would come to his assistance; far better to let a rival perish, for the males had their mates in cub and they had no wish to set free a possible rival. The sheep never even looked up for it could tell the difference between the bark of a dog and a fox. Had the noise been canine then it would have moved away; foxes did not trouble it.

Only the rabbits moved. Rak felt the vibration, heard the humming of the wire fence as the coneys jumped through the mesh squares and bolted for their warren in the wood. They had no need to use that gap beneath the bottom strand and, anyway, for a long time now it had smelled strongly of fox and badger. They had learned to avoid it.

The silence rolled back. Rak's body was becoming numb, he gave to barking again, a monotonous high pitched yelping which embodied fear and resignation to his fate. Eventually, that shepherd would come. Rak would cower, wait for the deafening report. He saw it, lived it, heard it a score of times, eventually he did not even flinch at the imagined approach, cringed and hoped that death would be quick.

Until those approaching footsteps became reality.

Rak lay there trembling. He scented fox but the smell permeated this crossing place between forest and dingle. Yet the footfalls were light and fast, not heavy and lumbering. Maybe it was a woodland fox returning from a hunt in the snowy pastures, intending to use this access to the forest. In which case when it saw Rak held firmly in the snare it would change course; the fence was an easy jump, it would pass him by, leave him to his fate.

Rak stared, made out the silhouette of a fox. Perhaps this was a figment of his exhausted and tortured imagination. In which case it might be Shi, but she could not help him because she was dead.

It wasn't Shi; he saw that much as the vixen came close,

recognized her scent, and had he still had the strength and voice he would have barked in joy.

It was Tosca.

Tosca came close, sniffed at him reassuringly. She had heard and recognized his bark, it had carried far in the still, freezing night air. Luckily, she had gone up to the entrance to the earth to await his return for he had been away a long time. She had set off in search of him forthwith.

She did not know if she could set him free, for she had never attempted to bite through a snare before. Rus had once; she had been with him on that particular occasion when they had come upon a half-grown fox caught in a gamekeeper's noose. That was in the days when they had inhabited Hopwas Wood; Jenkins had been the guardian of the game preserves then. The old man was kind to badgers but he showed no mercy towards foxes. Nobody did. But Rus had freed the captive, a naïve creature who had not lived long enough to learn by his mistake. Two nights later Jenkins had shot him on the edge of the wood at dusk.

Tosca's sharp teeth began probing Rak's neck in search of the noose; she found it, almost choked him as she loosened it enough to pull the wire between her jaws. Then she began to gnaw, sawing, grinding so that the sensation vibrated inside her head. A little fraying, a broken strand pricked her gum, almost made her lose her hold but she ignored the sharp pain.

Every so often she broke off to glance around her; she listened but the only noise was that of sheep pulling at the stiff grass. In severe weather they often fed in the night because there was insufficient time during the day to eat their fill of the frozen grass. There was no sound of human footsteps.

The sky was beginning to pale. There was an urgency now in the way Tosca bit at that stubborn woven steel wire; time was not on her side. With the approach of dawn she was able to view the results of her labours; a tangle of frayed strands but there was still a way to go. Frantically she renewed her efforts.

Rak lay there limply; at one stage she feared that he had died, but an eye flickered open, looked up at her. She tried to encourage him, snapped another strand. And another.

It was full daylight.

The crows were gliding out of the tall pines, cawing mournfully. Severe weather was a time of hardship for them; they circled, hoping that one of the hardy sheep left out to graze might have died in the night. But none had, so they flew on.

A cluster of woodpigeons broke from their roost wood. Their flight was fast for they had a long way to travel for their first feed of the day; there was a field of cabbages way beyond the village, its greenery poking up out of the encrusted snow. They would ravage the crop; the gas banger in the centre had long since ceased to alarm them, they had become used to its noise and learned that it did no harm.

Tosca grunted her satisfaction as the final strand of wire broke and the noose fell limply from Rak's chafed neck. He lay there, exhausted, unable to understand that he was free. She pulled at his shoulder with her aching teeth, helped him to crawl from beneath the fence. With difficulty he stood up; she leaned against him until the circulation flowed through his numbed limbs again.

Together they walked along the track beneath the firs, found the fork that headed them in the direction of Badger Wood. It was going to be a long slow journey home.

They would go hungry until night fell again on this arctic landscape, but that was a small price to pay for Rak's life.

Chapter Thirteen

The severe weather continued up until the end of January, bright sunshine by day and hard frosts by night. Some of the snow melted on the fir branches but the deep drifts remained solid and unyielding. It was a time of hardship for the birds and beasts of the wooded hills.

However, Rak, now fully recovered from his ordeal, benefited from the abundance of dying rabbits. As often happens, rabbits suffering from the latter stages of myxomatosis desert their burrows. Possibly those not infected drive them out for few wild creatures have compassion for one of their own species which is either weak or infirm. Or perhaps these coneys in discomfort become disorientated; blinded and deafened by their festering swellings, they awaited merciful death. Whatever the reasons, rabbits were often to be found crouched beneath snow-weighted bushes or lying stiff and cold in the below-freezing temperatures.

Rak brought many of these victims to Tosca in the warmth of the earth. In Winter food was scarce, you were grateful for anything that was edible.

The thaw came gradually. The biting wind changed direction, came from the south-west instead of the north-east, bringing with it a warmer, damper atmosphere. The drifts melted steadily by day, sometimes froze slightly by night when the temperature dropped, but gradually diminished. Gone was that beautiful virgin whiteness, the landscape became off-white, a slushy brown on tracks and forestry roads.

The stream down in the dingle, where Rak had suffered ignominy and terror in that wire noose, became a raging, foaming torrent and the river beyond the village burst its banks and flooded the meadows.

There was even a hint of Spring in the air, some of the shrubs sprouted new buds and the songbirds gave voice with relief. Winter was not gone but this was a welcome respite.

The crows were busy; one or two of the hardy sheep left to fend for themselves had perished in the snowdrifts; now the thaw exposed their carcasses, meat that was there for the scavenging. But Rak kept well clear of the carrion, he remembered only too well what had happened to Tika. A dead ewe might conceal a trap. Likewise, well-used runs through hedges and gaps in fences reminded him of a wire noose waiting to slip over his neck and tighten as he squeezed through. He was wary, knew that he lacked the experience and cunning of his wild cousins who had long learned to survive in a land where Man was hostile towards them. His fear, his caution, was depriving the two foxes of food that was so necessary to them.

There were hardly any rabbits to be seen. The freezing temperatures had wiped out those inflicted with the disease, but the survivors had huddled in their burrows and the plague-carrying fleas had infected them, too. In close confinement the virus had incubated at an alarming rate and by the time the thaw came most of these had contracted myxomatosis and died below ground.

Just a handful of coneys remained immune to the lingering death. They seemed to sense that the continuation of their species depended upon their own survival so they took to remaining below ground more than usual. Their habits changed; they fed before dusk and after dawn, the night hours were too perilous to be abroad. Consequently, they were seldom seen by those nocturnal predators for whom they were a staple diet. Both Pyne and Sacko had diversified; they took to raiding the farmlands in the valley, plundered free-ranging poultry and semi-tame pheasants on the game preserves. The uplands were no longer a land of plenty for the carnivores.

Times were changing.

Tosca was heavy with her cubs, it would only be a matter of a week or two before she gave birth; she dared not risk a hunting foray. In any case, she would be too cumbersome for a stalk or chase. As there were not enough rabbits to provide regular sustenance, so Rak must diversify just as the polecat and the stoat had done. The badgers were more fortunate, they could live on pig nuts and beechmast which had lain preserved beneath the icy snowdrifts, and they knew how to take hedgehogs without being spiked.

First, she told Rak, he must risk the dead sheep. There *might* be traps set, but a wary fox would spot all but the most cunningly concealed ones. Usually the shepherds and farmers hid them beneath a layer of wool ripped from the body. So beware, tread only on exposed patches of ground. Note where other predators had fed in safety and feed there; then tear off the meat in strips and bring her some.

Rak set off just after dark, squeezed through dense hawthorn rather than use an inviting gap, and jumped mesh fences instead of going under them. The ground was soft, squelchy and waterlogged in places after the thaw. He made wide detours as Tosca had instructed him, always travelled into the wind but took care to approach the sheep fields from below, for surely traps or snares set to catch an unwary fox would have been placed in anticipation of the intended victim travelling from the deep woods. An approach from below was safer.

It took much longer than usual to reach those pastures where he had seen two dead sheep the night before. He stood on top of a rise, looked down and searched the tussocky field for those carcasses. One had lain about twenty yards from the hedge on his left, the other had been in the middle.

There was no sign of either.

His first thought was that he had come to the wrong field, he still had difficulty in finding his way about in this landscape.

No, it was the field for which he had searched, he recognized the stunted pine that grew in the far corner. So where had the dead sheep gone? Neither corvids nor foxes would have been capable of cleaning up the entire carrion, skeletons would have remained to whiten in the elements.

There was wool everywhere, tufts scattered across the grass, caught up in the thistles. Rak approached warily, circled at a distance. That was when he came upon the tracks; twin patterned tyre marks that had sunk into the ground; in places the wheels had spun, squirted mud in all directions.

Rak was familiar with vehicles, the rubbery scent that tyres left behind. He also knew that vehicles took things away. This one had collected the dead sheep, transported them to another place.

He felt frustration, despair. The rabbits were no more, only a few healthy ones which he would be extremely lucky to catch, and now the plentiful carrion had been removed. What else was left to him?

His thoughts switched to the village below. There were dustbins behind the big house but if anyone heard you, then you could expect a hail of leaden death from those sticks that banged. It was a risk but you risked everything when your only choice was death by starvation or shooting. In between there was a remote chance of survival so you took it.

Rak turned, cantered in the direction of the village down in the valley.

The terrain levelled, the fields had an artificiality about them; hedgerows were few and far between, the land was divided by mesh fences with barbed wire strands on top, every square metre of each field was utilized for maximum production whether it was lush grass for sheep and cattle or neatly ploughed arable awaiting the sowing of Spring crops. Hedges obscured valuable sunlight, the original hawthorn had been bulldozed out; there were drainage ditches so that the ground did not become waterlogged, steel gates instead of the rickety wooden ones on higher ground. There were no tussocks, patches of thistles or rough corners in which a rabbit might have hidden.

Rak had not noticed any of this on his travels up to the wooded hills, now it was all too apparent. Man had conquered the lower ground, this was no place for animals who might hinder his obsession for commercial farming.

To an urban fox who was struggling to integrate into a new environment, this was yet another alien landscape.

Rak was wary; even in the dead of night he sensed the hostility, there were surely traps and snares set in case fox or badger should dare to trespass here. Where once he had been homesick for his native city, now he longed for the hills, the woods which offered sanctuary to a hunted creature, and Tosca who knew the ways of Nature and would teach him to survive.

But Tosca was not here with him and there was no way she could make the long journey in her condition. They were both in need of food and it was his duty to provide for them.

Which was why he continued across those neatly cultivated fields, until he came to the whitewashed farmhouse enclosed by a concrete yard and a gate which stood invitingly open.

He crouched in a patch of shadow. There were tall barns behind the house, stacked with bales of hay and straw which smelled sweet in the night air. A tractor stood like some slumbering monster guarding an implements shed, and there were more sheds, the original buildings behind the new ones. He noted a ramshackle dog kennel in a far corner, a rusted chain coiled in front of the entrance. At least there was no dog here to growl and bark and raise the alarm.

There were sure to be some dustbins close to the house; Rak checked to ensure that none of the windows were lighted. The occupants were sleeping. He moved across into the yard. So long as he was quick, did not make a noise . . .

Something moved above his head, had him drawing back instinctively, ready to flee. He looked up, stared in amazement at what he saw.

Perched on the six-foot-high wall, some huddled together, others spaced out at varying intervals, was a line of birds. Big ones, small ones, colours that either stood out starkly in the half light or else blended into camouflaged insignificance. They shuffled nervously on their roost, some of the gaps were closing up as the uneasy birds sought safety in huddled numbers.

Rak was reminded of the pigeons and starlings which roosted nightly on the high ledges and roofs of the old buildings in the city, twittering hordes that bombed late night revellers with their foul droppings.

But even the smallest of these were too big for pigeons, their colourings weren't right either. Nor was their scent, a smell that reminded him of chicken carcasses amongst the dustbins.

A bantam hen clucked her fear, nestled up to an Old

English cockerel with spectacular red, black and yellow plumage. He remained motionless except for a fast blinking of eyes that saw and understood. By day he ruled the farmyard; his sharp talons had raked the feathers of many a would-be challenger; he had put many a troublesome Collie to flight. By night he sought the safety of this high wall for often he had watched smugly as his most feared predators prowled the perimeter; he had not seen Rus for a while now, but both Sacko and Pyne had visited during the hard weather. During the weeks whilst the snow had lain on the ground, Buster had roosted his flock up in the hay bales for warmth but with the coming of the thaw he had returned his charges to the outer yard. This wall was smooth with age, there was no foothold to assist a climbing poultry hunter. They were safe enough here, weren't they? Suddenly he had his doubts.

The hen clucked again, pushed up against Buster. The others were starting to crowd him. A Silky-cross fluttered to regain its foothold on the slippery surface, they were all looking to Buster for protection.

Rak tensed, muzzle uplifted. So near and yet so far, twice the height of the sheep fencing which he had cleared with ease on the journey here. He recalled that tall blue brick wall beyond the tunnel that led away from the railway embankment where not even a clump of wild willow herb nor a birch sapling could find a hold, the awesomeness of that unclimbable sheer surface. He had fled from it then because it gave him a trapped feeling. As did this farmyard now with its walled perimeter, too high to jump, the only visible exit the open gateway into the rutted, muddy lane.

Rak would have turned and fled except that he was hungry.

A sudden leap, a powering of his back legs, springboarded by sheer desperation. If he failed, then all was lost. Outstretched paws, mouth agape, poised to snap and hold.

He caught Buster, the ageing cockerel, by a scaly leg,

arched his back as he started to slip; frantic wingbeats slapped his face as he fell but somehow he held on. Falling, turning in mid-air, bracing himself for the impact when he hit the ground.

He rolled, maintained his bite on that leg, felt it break. Buster was screeching, trying to tear himself free. Rak almost lost his grip, found it again, tasted blood as a sharp talon raked his tongue. Wingbeats all around him, frantic crowing and clucking, birds flying blindly into unseen obstructions, thumping to the ground. Running.

Maybe Rus would have quickly despatched his catch, gone after the others; an unholy spree of decapitations, headless bodies flapping their last in his wake, a bloodlust that would only subside when every fowl in the farmyard was either dead or beyond his reach. Then, and only then, would he have picked up his chosen kill and departed swiftly.

But Rak lacked that instinct to slaughter wantonly. He had hunted and caught because he and Tosca were starving, for no other reason. Cockerel wings slapped his face, obscured his vision. He killed quickly so that he might see the way out to freedom. Feathers floated in the night breeze, he dropped the twitching bird, secured a better grip on it and fled out through the gateway.

Behind him the noise of the frightened poultry was growing fainter; he thought he heard angry human voices, a dog starting to bark. But they would not catch Rak now, he took the first fence in his easy, loping stride, did not even bother to look back.

He had much to tell Tosca; of how he had dodged the many traps and snares set for him, of his cunning infiltration of Man's domain, of that death-defying leap in which he had secured this bird which had roosted with apparent immunity in a human stronghold.

For he was Rak, king of the foxes, hunter supreme, a

Nimrod, nemesis of smaller creatures of the countryside. Even the badgers feared him, for did they not avoid him on their travels? Such was his invincibility that he would return to that farm again and again, night after night, and plunder those birds which roosted on the wall until, like the rabbits of the fields and woods, none remained.

Dawn was breaking when Rak and Tosca shared that bird in the safety of the earth, feasting ravenously until only the bones and a pile of feathers remained. And afterwards they slept contentedly.

Chapter Fourteen

The false Spring fooled even the wildlife which had experienced mild weather in the depths of Winter in the past. The rooks always built their nests in the topmost branches of the tallest trees in early February and that never ceased to encourage their cousins, the jays and magpies, to follow their example. The woodpigeon sat her eggs for most of the year, regularly lost clutches in cold weather due to her own foolishness. She never gave up, started all over again.

Down on the game preserves, Reuben, the gamekeeper, had already collected his first pheasant egg. Unseasonal climatic conditions had shrubs coming into bud when there would be severe frosts to nip them off, chicks hatched with no hope of survival. But the vixens gave birth regardless of the weather because the time was right for them, and they had snug warmth in their earths.

The warm prevailing winds swung round to the north, took on a biting edge with the change of direction. A few clear, frosty days and nights followed before the skies clouded, became leaden and spat flurries of snow. This time, though, it was no vicious blizzard, instead a light sugary covering that crunched beneath the tread of Man and beast on the hard ground. Forests of lightly dusted Christmas trees on the hillsides had a festive look about them that was a reminder of the season past.

Tosca had her litter, five healthy cubs, on that starry night when Rak returned from a foray to the farm with a brace of bantams. Luck was with him; the cold weather had prompted the poultry to return to the hay barns but two of the birds had unwisely roosted on some low bales. Rak had leaped for a leg, discovered that he had caught two! Euphoric, he had dashed from the yard with both bantams fluttering in his mouth, left a trail of multi-coloured feathers in his wake.

The sheepdog which was kept chained in the porch had been late to bark for he had been sleeping heavily after a hard day's work. By the time the upper windows were lighted and a head poked out there was nothing to see. The farmer cursed his dog for a false alarm and went back to his bed. Lambing time was nigh, he had more important things on his mind than poultry. He had noticed, however, that their numbers had diminished considerably and there was an abundance of feathers in the farmyard.

Rak was determined to go on raiding the farm as long as there were birds for the taking. It was more difficult now that the assortment of bantams had taken to roosting in inaccessible places but there would always be the odd one which had chosen a vulnerable perch for the night. And if it should so happen that every one of them was beyond reach, then they always dropped down to breakfast on the granary spillings at first light . . .

A ewe had lambed in the dingle. She had wandered away from the rest of the small flock, found a sheltered hollow close to the path that followed the winding course of the rushing hill stream. She gave birth during the night hours;

twins, one was healthy, tottering on its feet within the hour, the other was sickly and lay close to her. If it had wanted to feed then it had not the strength to lift its head to suckle.

By daylight the ewe was in difficulties; the after-birth had not come away, she started a fever. The one lamb was dead, the other was having trouble feeding because its mother lay awkwardly.

Some crows watched from a line of silver birches on the brow of the snowy bank. They had seen it all before, knew it was only a matter of time before they would be able to swoop down on the dead and the dying. They were in no hurry. Others joined them, sinister black birds, harbingers of death, gregarious like desert vultures. When their comrades clustered, perched silently without so much as a raucous *caw*, then there was carrion in the offing. There would be plenty for all.

The shepherd made a cursory check of his hill flock towards mid-morning; they were not due to lamb for another ten days yet, it was just a question of making sure that none had got their heads stuck in the mesh fence adjoining the forestry.

He checked the fox snare which he kept set in the gap beneath the fence. It was untouched, nothing had passed this way during the night. He was unlikely, though, to catch that fox again which had bitten its way to freedom, it would be wary of this place. But there were plenty of foxes in the forest, he might have better luck tomorrow.

He did not trouble to count his sheep this morning for they were scattered amongst the scrub on the banks of the dingle. Tomorrow he would make a head count. They were sure to be all right. He needed to return to the farm down below where some premature lambing had already started; there were always the odd one or two that came early.

The ewe in the bottom of the dingle lay at full stretch, her weight crushing her dead offspring. Her eyes were closed. Nearby the other lamb bleated pitifully.

The waiting corvids stretched their wings. It was almost time.

Rak found the dead sheep and her lambs two nights later. The second lamb had died from a combination of cold and starvation. The crows had fed well but there was enough meat remaining on the two small stripped carcasses for himself and Tosca.

The following night he returned to see what he could salvage from the ewe. He made a cautious approach, walked on the side of the animal track that led down from the forest to the dingle fence. He knew that a fresh wire had been set in the gap in the mesh, that was no problem. The ground was higher on the wood side of the fence, a jump was easy. All he had to do then was to ensure that there were no traps set around the dead sheep.

He emerged from the trees, began the descent of the steep bank. The reflection of the lying snow made it easy to discern outlines; he saw the taut squares of the fence, the strand of barbed wire above it. Then he tensed as he sensed a movement, a stirring and rustling, a vibration of the taut wire. Something clinked, rattled. It was a familiar sound, one which he would never forget, the noise of a steel swivel which anchored a fox snare to a fence post being jangled as a captive animal moved.

Rak drew back, wary, ready to turn and flee. The hollow beneath the fence was in darkness but a shape that was blacker than the enshrouding shadow moved, checked. It pulled; Rak heard a choking sound, a spitting and snarling.

A fox was caught in the snare!

Rak moved closer, careful to keep his distance. But even his own reasoning told him if a fox was already ensnared, then there was little danger to himself. All the same, he must take a look. It wouldn't be Tosca, she would not have left the cubs unattended in the earth.

He had to ascertain the identity of the captive creature. In all probability it was some wild hill fox whose alertness had lapsed due to the hardships and hunger during a spell of severe weather.

It definitely wasn't a vixen, the pungent stench of dog fox was overwhelming. It also embodied the terror of a trapped animal, its desperation to fight to the death. That was why Rak approached warily.

The other hissed a warning, it did not even trust one of its own kind. The wire tautened again, the captive choked; Rak knew that it was frothing at the mouth, the way he himself had done that time. He knew what it was going through; in the end it would give up the struggle, resign itself to a lingering death.

He had been fortunate, Tosca had heard his barking and come to his rescue. This fox was lucky, also, because Rak had chanced to travel this way. But Rak did not know whether he would have the strength to gnaw through the closely stranded wire. It had taken Tosca an eternity to free him.

He took another step forward but a warning hiss halted him. The other bared its fangs, saliva strung from them. And in that instant recognition was mutual.

The snared fox was none other than Rus!

Rak experienced a feeling of pity. Surely Rus's awareness, his alertness, had deserted him, for the old dog fox had survived Man's attempts to kill him throughout his lifetime. Now, dulled by age, he had blundered into a snare just as the inexperienced Rak had done. Tosca had freed Rak, now it was up to Rak to give Rus his liberty back.

Rus lay silent, the shadows were too deep for Rak to read

the expression in his eyes but it might have been one of relief, of gratitude.

Rak moved close to the other, his teeth ready to probe for the cutting snare in the same way that he hunted lice in his own fur. The noose was doubtless around Rus's neck; as soon as he located it he would begin to bite and grind on the wire, sawing patiently until the strands frayed and parted. It would be a long task but he needed to complete it by daylight before the shepherd came to inspect his wire.

Suddenly Rus's head turned, his teeth snapped, bit Rak sharply on the cheek. Shock and pain had the younger fox leaping back, hissing angrily at this act of ingratitude. His face hurt, he tasted blood on his lip.

Rus was angry now, not with Man who had trapped him but with this arrogant dog fox who was not only, it seemed, gloating over defeating him in the battle for a life-long mate but now wished to humble him further by rescuing him from Man! He, Rus, would never accept the friendship of a rival, he would not be beholden to a usurper. He would not give Rak the opportunity to boast of how he had not only defeated the legendary Rus in combat but had also saved his life. Better to die than to be ridiculed amongst the hill foxes.

Rak did not understand the pride of the wild foxes, it did not make sense to him. He tried to reason with the other but Rus hissed angrily, would have leaped for his throat had not the strainer wire restricted him. He backed away in order not to risk another bite.

Perhaps he could go and get help, Tosca might be able to leave her cubs for a short while . . .

Rus flew into a frenzy, straining at the snare, oblivious of how it throttled him until he had to drop back in order to breathe. He would not accept help from Tosca, either, nor any of the other foxes. There was one small favour he would ask, though. Would Rak forget that he had come upon the noble Rus caught in a snare? Rus had not been seen for a long time, after tomorrow he would not be sighted again. Let those tales of daring, of how he had outwitted Man and dogs on innumerable occasions, live on. All he asked, pleaded, was that Rus should disappear for ever. Perhaps he had travelled on to another domain far from here, and on moonlit nights he still hunted the rabbits on the moor. Or else, maybe, he had died of old age, and Man could never boast of defeating him. At least, if nobody knew the truth, then Rus would die in peace, the suffering would only be short lived, and he would be happy that way.

Rak agreed reluctantly. He would do as the other asked, he would not even tell Tosca for she would be angry with him for not freeing her former mate. Wouldn't she? Rus appeared to think that she would be more angry if Rak gnawed through the wire – for she would understand. But he would rather she did not know. Let Rak go on his way– he sank back down to the ground – and forget that he had ever seen Rus this one last time.

Sadly, Rak leaped the fence and trotted on down to where the remains of the dead ewe lay strewn across the flattened, frozen undergrowth. There was no meat left for himself and Tosca and the cubs.

Tonight he must venture back to the farm in the valley and plunder the surviving bantams.

Chapter Fifteen

*R*ak sensed that something was wrong even before he slunk in through the farmyard gate. A scent that was more a feeling than a smell in the atmosphere, a stillness that transcended the silence of a rural night. Perhaps had it not been for Tosca and the cubs he would have suffered his own hunger and turned back. But all that was left to him were the roosting bantams.

He kept to the shadows cast by the buildings, looked towards the house to ensure that no windows were lighted. He glanced over to the perimeter wall; there were no birds roosting there who might have been snatched by the leg with a sudden leap. No dog barked from the porch.

It was as if everything was just waiting for something to happen.

A movement across the yard attracted his attention, as if the frozen ground was rippling. He tensed, listened. There was only silence.

Then he saw what it was that moved. *Feathers*. Bunches of them blowing in the soft breeze, wafting, floating. Settling. There were always feathers to be found in a farmyard where poultry roamed free but not in this quantity. They were scattered in all directions, caught up against the wheels of the tractor, piling in corners in the way of drifting snow.

Then he saw the corpses, mutilated birds lying on their backs, wings outspread, breasts stained scarlet. A dozen or more scattered around the foot of the hay barn. Rak stared, unable to understand what had happened until a bounding movement at the far end caught his eye. Something that ran jerkily, stopped once to look back at him. At first he thought it was Sacko but the body was too large, too furry. It passed through a patch of starlight briefly and that was when Rak recognized his fellow intruder in this farmyard.

It was Pyne. The polecat had slaughtered wantonly and now he was departing, dragging a dead bantam cockerel in his mouth.

Rak watched the other disappear and then turned his attention to the dead poultry. There were enough birds here to feed his family for days if only he could have transported them back to the earth. Maybe he could carry two, even three, but it was too far, too risky, to return for more. And after tonight there would be nothing left to come back here for.

Rak moved out from the shadows, the nearest bantam was lying twenty yards away with some more close by. He would gather as many as he could, flee with his burden. At least the cubs would not go hungry tonight. Maybe tomorrow Tosca would have an idea where an alternative food supply might be found.

Rak was within a yard of the motionless birds when the entire yard lit up. A blinding light rendered him sightless in a second; a glare, so powerful that he knew it did not come from the farmhouse windows, turned night into instant day; even the sun could not shine with such brightness. And yet there was no warmth.

He might have fled except that he was rendered motionless, a loss of direction and understanding, confusion and fear.

And then pain.

It was as if dozens of barbs from the strand on top of the forestry fence had pierced him simultaneously, burned deep and thrown him sideways with unbelievable force. He rolled, was aware of a deafening explosion. More pain and then another crashing bang.

He writhed, twisted, somehow regained his feet. He went down on his forelegs, sheer desperation and fear lifted him back up. The pain was unbearable, he cried out. He could not see, that light seared his eyes with cold fire. He ran blindly, stumbling, not knowing in which direction he was going, not caring.

He knew the pain had come from a gun because he recognized the resonant bangs. Whatever missiles it threw had hit him, splattered all over his body, burned him in many different places. But no limbs were broken, he could still run.

His head hit something solid with a sickening crunch and he slumped to the ground. Momentary unconsciousness; but he revived, found himself following the wall, leaning on it for support. Until it was no longer there and he knew that he had found the gateway.

The darkness revived him further and he could see again. A powerful beam of light was arcing over him but the farm wall shielded him. He ran down the rutted track until he felt tarmac beneath his pads, knew that if he crossed the road then he would be in the field.

A dog was barking back at the farm but it was not pursuing him. For some reason whoever had shot him had not unleashed the collie that was chained in the porch. Sheepdogs were not fighters, perhaps its owner feared for its safety if he loosed it in pursuit of a wounded fox.

Rak knew that he was bleeding, it was a frightening sen-

sation. Maybe had he still been a loner, an urban fox abandoned in the wilds, he would have lain down and waited to
die. But he remembered Tosca and the cubs; he had to find
them, to be with them. That was all that mattered, the force
that drove him on when the strength was ebbing from his
body; he left a trail of blood in his wake.

Somehow he made it to the top of the first field. His vision
darkened, he felt dizzy. His legs would scarcely bear the
weight of his shot-lacerated body so he lowered it gently
down on the hard frozen surface. The relief at being able to
rest for a few minutes rallied him. He twisted his head
around, licked at his wounds; they smarted, oozed blood.
There were those which he was unable to reach and he felt
the blood soaking the fur around them.

The temptation was to stretch out, close his eyes, and, in
spite of the pain, he might have slept. But he knew that he
must not tarry here long, if his strength ebbed he might not
be able to get back on to his feet and then he would never
make it back to the earth.

It was a struggle to stand upright again. He tottered
unsteadily, almost fell. Only sheer willpower enabled him to
move his feet. From here on it was all uphill, the going was
arduous but he knew that he must not rest again.

It was dawn by the time he reached the dingle and drank
gratefully from the rushing torrent. The icy water slaked his
burning thirst, seemed to ease his smarting wounds.

He passed by the place where the sheep and her ewes had
died, just skeletons now with wool strewn across the frozen
bracken. He knew that he would be unable to jump the
forestry fence, perhaps there was another gap further along.
The snared Rus blocked the only entrance which Rak knew;
maybe he could persuade his rival to allow him to squeeze
by. Rus had refused help but surely he would not obstruct a
wounded fox?

Rus was lying beneath the fence. The sky was beginning to pale now and Rak could just make out the other's outline against the background. Rus did not move; it seemed as though he had given up his struggles, had conceded defeat at the cruel hands of Man, awaiting the shepherd's coming and the blissful release from his agonies. Rak knew only too well how the other felt.

Rak approached cautiously. The trapped fox's scent had a staleness about it, it no longer reeked of an aggressive male, that secretion which was a prelude to snapping jaws. Rak hesitated, he dared not approach too close until he knew how Rus would react.

Rus did not move, his head was not lifted up off the ground, his ears did not prick up. Rak stopped; maybe the other slept, exhausted from his struggles. He risked another unsteady step forward. Only then did he know why Rus, the mighty hunter, king of the hill foxes, did not stir.

Because Rus was dead. The trauma of finding himself snared after years of outwitting Man, the titanic struggles of an ageing body had proved too much for him. His heart had given out, brought blissful relief from pain and anguish.

Rak managed to squeeze past the still form, struggled to drag himself through the narrowed gap beneath the fence. He felt a sense of sadness for he had never borne a grudge against the other. Rus had been a fine fox in his day, the nemesis of shepherds and farmers, a spectre whom huntsmen and hounds had pursued with futility, time after time. Finally, this ageing outlaw, a legend amongst foxes, had perished ignominiously in a snare set by a shepherd. Rus deserved a better end, a death worthy of the life he had lived.

Rak found the narrow track, followed it until he came to where it forked, and began the long trek back up to Badger Wood. In places the ground was so steep that he faltered, found himself stepping backwards. His pain-ravaged body cried out for rest but he denied it relentlessly. If he lay down, he would never rise again.

Suddenly it was full daylight; through his fogged vision he was aware that the stars were gone and the rosy rays of an early morning sun were slanting down through the criss-crossed branches overhead. It was not far now, and he knew he would make it; he recognized the stunted oak that grew outside the wood, knew that the fox earth was beyond the first rise.

He staggered, it was all he could do to remain upright. A familiar well-trodden track that led right up to the entrance to his underground lair.

Ten yards. Less. Something moved at the extremity of his restricted range of vision and he knew without any doubt that it was Tosca standing outside the earth, a vixen who had fretted this past hour because her mate had not returned from his hunting trip.

Then she was by his side, her lean body against his own so that he could support himself against her, asking no questions because she guessed only too well what Man had done to him.

Chapter Sixteen

Rak knew that he was back in the earth because Tosca was by his side, licking his wounds with her rough tongue and the cubs were milling about, climbing all over him, biting his ears. He couldn't see but below ground it was always dark; you relied upon your senses, you scented, you heard and you felt. You did not need your eyesight.

He could not remember how he came to be here, perhaps he had never left, it was just one of those dreams and when you awoke everything would be as it had always been, nothing would have changed. But it wasn't a dream, the pain all over his body was a burning reality which denied him sleep.

Tosca snapped at the cubs, warned them to be still. They huddled in a corner, frightened; then they began to play a game of their own, chasing one another's tails. Shrill yelps denoted when one was caught.

Tosca went outside the earth, she could no longer bear to watch Rak suffer. She knew from the moment when she first set eyes on the injured Rak that he would not live. On two previous occasions she had come across wounded foxes after the shepherds had beaten through the woods with dogs to drive the foxes out to the waiting guns.

Those foxes which were killed outright were the lucky ones, a brief moment of pain and then came merciful oblivion. She and Rus, however, had long ago learned how to outwit the humans on these hunts; you ran forward in front of the dogs and then, using wind direction to your advantage, you circled back, a wide detour which brought you out behind the beaters. All you had to do then was to return to where you had been lying up originally and you were safe. The men never seemed to think of looking for foxes *behind* the lines.

But the worst fate of all was to be shot and wounded at a long distance; a stinging pain but it didn't drop you, didn't stop you running. Once Tosca had watched a fox bowled over by a salvo of shots. It had rolled, picked itself up and carried on as though it was completely unscathed.

Two nights afterwards, whilst out hunting, Rus and Tosca had happened upon that same fox lying in a sheltered hollow deep in the woods. Its eyes had pleaded for death; if either Tosca or her mate had been capable of despatching it and ending its suffering, they would have done so.

Its tongue hung limply out of its mouth, bleeding from where it had been bitten at the height of the poor creature's agony. Its fur was matted, a score of pellet wounds were still seeping blood. It had a fever, too, because those shot wounds had begun to fester.

That fox lingered another whole day and finally died during the following night.

Rak's whole body burned, his tongue lolled out in desperate need of water but the only place to drink was the stream in the dingle. There was no way he could travel the distance to that thirst-quenching brook; likewise, Tosca was incapable of bringing him water. So his thirst raged.

He was sure that he could hear an approaching train, feel the ground begin to tremble long before the clattering line of trucks was within earshot. A rumbling and rattling; he tensed with joy and disbelief. His relief escalated to euphoria.

Everything *was* all right, he was home on his beloved railway embankment and it was Shi who was comforting him. He was ill; he had never been ill in his life before, it was very frightening. He had slept and dreamed a long and terrifying dream about a faraway land inhabited by strange and vicious creatures, foxes who were not like the foxes he knew here. He and Shi had been parted, they had wandered lost for a very long time but somehow they had managed to find their way back to the city.

And it did not really matter because they had never actually been away from here. He could not understand how his body came to be hurting this way, but Shi could tell him.

Her answer was puzzling. She spoke of sticks that made loud bangs and inflicted pain and injury, sometimes death. And she told him how Man was the fox's enemy, how he would kill them all if he could.

It did not make sense; the humans put out food in their gardens for the foxes during cold weather, they never harmed them. Shi must be mistaken, something else must have happened to him.

Rak had been run down by a train, that was the only answer! Those relentless wheels had lacerated his body but somehow he had lived.

But he was happy in spite of his suffering because he was back in his beloved homeland. He had never wanted to be anywhere else. Shi had given birth to a litter he was proud of. As soon as he was better he would move out of the earth, lie up in the undergrowth close by and keep a watchful eye

128

on his mate and her offspring. He would bring them food from the dustbins, guard over them when the street dogs came to make a nuisance of themselves. At least there were no fierce animals with striped heads or foxes like Rus.

He might have dozed, he did not really know, but some time later the wounds weren't hurting any more. He wasn't thirsty, either. He almost felt as if he could stand up, walk up the tunnel to the world above but he decided against it. The cubs were sleeping in a heap close by, snoring contentedly, and it was his duty to look after them.

It must be night and Shi had probably gone out into the streets to scavenge from the dustbins; she would be sure to bring him something, a half-eaten chicken carcass, maybe, which the humans had wasted. He might feel better still once he had eaten. He thought about going up above to wait for her on top of the earth. No, it wasn't a good idea, she would be angry with him for leaving the litter unattended.

Was that another train passing by? He could not be sure but it was bound to be; trains travelled along the line below the embankment many times during the course of a day.

He felt *so* tired, but he knew he was well again. Shi's tongue had remarkable healing powers, he remembered a long time ago, one very hot summer, when he had cut his pad on a piece of broken glass. She had licked it for hours and eventually it had stopped bleeding. Two days later he was able to walk on that foot.

Tomorrow, Rak decided, he would take a walk down to the railway line, find a patch of undergrowth and lie there and watch the trains go by.

He stretched himself out, rested his head on his paws, and closed his eyes.

And slept.

Afterword

After Rak died, Tosca set about raising her litter all on her own. No other dog fox would come to her assistance, it was too late in the year. They would only take an interest in her in the Autumn when she called and the cycle was ready to begin all over again.

Each night she left the cubs unattended and went in search of food. Rabbits were breeding in the big warren beneath the blackberry bushes in Badger Wood. Each night these creatures followed the same route out to feed on the sheep fields. They were easily ambushed.

The badgers objected to this poaching on what they considered to be their hunting territory. Once Shaf had lain in wait for Tosca, and had charged down on her ferociously but she was much too nimble for her irate attacker.

However, she decided to avoid trespassing in the badgers' domain in future. Her concern was not for her own safety but for that of her offspring, for the badgers might visit the fox earth in her absence and kill her cubs. Her neighbours were vengeful when aroused, it was a risk she could not take.

The cubs grew quickly. By Midsummer they should have left the earth, forsaken their mother and gone their separate ways. Strangely, they didn't, although they went off foraging each night, they always returned home. Hungry.

It was some time before Tosca realized that her young were not eating enough to satisfy their growing bodies. They were very thin, their bone structure was clearly visible beneath their matted coats, and their fur was far from glossy, because they lacked the necessary vitamins and protein to make them strong and healthy.

Tosca's maternal instinct warned her of this deficiency in the young foxes. It was against the laws of Nature for a vixen to hunt for food for her young when they were more than half grown. Nevertheless, Tosca knew that unless she provided for them they would almost certainly die.

The rabbits were making a comeback after their numbers had been decimated by the previous Winter's myxomatosis outbreak, the survivors had begun to breed again in an attempt to repopulate the woods, and there were plenty of young, naïve rabbits to be had for the taking. Tosca's first task was to feed her cubs, then she must teach them how to hunt for themselves.

Night after night she took rabbits on the edge of the wood, saw to it that her litter fed well. Within a couple of weeks they were showing signs of putting on weight, no longer were their rib-cages protruding through their coats. Now they must kill for themselves.

She remembered how she had tried to teach Rak to hunt. She had been shocked by his ignorance of the use of wind direction and cover; his stalks had been clumsy, alerting the feeding conies long before he was within reach of them. And when he finally made his first catch, the kill had been a clumsy and messy business.

So it was with these young foxes. Even small rabbits,

innocent of the ways of their predators, scampered back into cover long before the foxes were upon them. Tosca tried to teach them but her charges seemed unable to understand the rudiments of hunting for their food.

She took them out individually, made the other four sit and wait at a distance where any scent or noise which they might make would not disturb their intended prey.

Always it was Tosca, with the dawn beginning to lighten the night sky, who caught as many rabbits as was possible before they returned to their warren, so that her young might not spend the day with empty stomachs.

Rak would have fared no better without a supply of sickly rabbits and dead sheep, she knew that only too well. He had been fortunate otherwise she would have had to hunt for both of them. The poultry down at the farm had been easy prey but in the end they had been his undoing.

She feared for the welfare of her grown litter. No matter how hard she attempted to instruct them in the art of survival, they seemed incapable of grasping the basics which should have been instinctive to any fox.

They appeared to lack that wariness which was the difference between living and dying. Once she had watched them, hunting in a pack like the dogs from down in the village, seemingly oblivious of a farmer who was inspecting his sheep prior to shearing.

Fortunately for the foxes, the stick which he carried was nothing more insidious than a shepherd's crook, cut and fashioned from an ash tree. He waved it, shouted, but the creatures of whom Tosca was becoming increasingly ashamed, merely stood and looked at him in surprise.

With the lushness of the undergrowth, the litter deserted Tosca. She had provided for them when they needed it most but now they rejected the mother who fed them.

Tosca did not see them again.

When the leaves began to fall, she called for a mate but her screams lacked the urgency and desperation of a younger vixen. For a long time her cries went unanswered until finally a dog fox appeared on the outskirts of Badger Wood.

Tosca recognized him as Rul, one whom Rus had driven from these parts some seasons ago. Hearing of his feared rival's death, Rul had returned to the territory which he had once coveted.

It was he who told Tosca of the deaths of some young foxes, stupid creatures who had perished at the jaws of the hounds on those early season forays prior to the serious business of fox hunting. Three had been killed on one pasture; they had not resorted to flight until the hounds were almost upon them, even the huntsmen had sat and stared in amazement.

The farmer who kept a few poultry down by the village had shot two more prowling his yard in broad daylight. There were other reports, Rul had heard, of foxes devoid of cunning being killed in the proximity of human habitation.

Rul had actually set eyes upon one of these unwary creatures on his travels. It had been thin, as if it had not eaten for weeks, a weakling who would doubtless be killed in combat if it challenged for a mate. Maybe that one, too, was dead by now, he had not heard.

The toll which humans took of foxes was worrying, Rul confided. There were always casualties, it was part of the game you played with Man; you always hoped that it would not be you who was killed. The huntsmen on horseback occasionally ran down a fox, but more often than not the pursued used his cunning and threw the pack of dogs off the scent, perhaps travelled up a stream so that the hounds wasted valuable time trying to ascertain where their quarry had climbed the opposite bank.

The men with guns took the heaviest toll; it was early in

the season yet but there were rumours in the hills of near massacres, a dozen or more foxes being accounted for in one drive.

There were road deaths, too, a rarity in the past but Rul had seen two himself on the narrow lanes that climbed up from the village below.

And, most worrying of all, Rul had come upon a dead fox in Badger Wood only recently. There was no mark on it, neither dog nor gun had killed it; it had just lain down and died. Foxes died of old age, if they were cunning enough to survive a lifetime, but this one was no more than a cub of the year and so pathetically thin that it was almost as though it had perished of starvation. That could not possibly be the case in these hills which now abounded with rabbits once more.

Could it?

Rul stayed around for only a short time. When Tosca called again there was no answering bark, no stealthy approach through the surrounding undergrowth. Away in the distance other vixens were calling, their lure was greater than that of an ageing female who, in all probability, would not be able to bear a litter the following Spring.

Tosca was sad that Rul had gone but she was not surprised. He was truly wild, he had all the cunning of a real hill fox; wherever he went his offspring would carry the genes that would enable them to hunt for food and survive Man's continued onslaught on the species. Would that he had answered her calling last Autumn and then her litter might have lived to see the coming Winter.

Yet she was secretly glad that she would not be able to breed again for she feared for the future of her own kind. Rak had died because he had been unable to survive away from the only habitat he knew. Without her he would have perished a long time ago. His offspring had been born to die. And there would be many more; Rul had spoken of an inferior breed.

She would not be sorry when her time came.